PURGATORY

CAROL SABEL BLODGETT
& L.M. PRATT

Purgatory

This is a work of fiction. Names, characters, businesses, places, events, locales, and incidents are either the products of the authors' imaginations or used in a fictitious manner. Any resemblance to actual persons, living or dead, or actual events is purely coincidental.

ISBN-13: 978-1-7324807-4-2

Cover design: Tatiana Villa, www.viladesign.net/

MYSTIC FORCES

BOOK II

PURGATORY

1

E L I A S

So this is what it's like.

I've never woken up beside a woman. I've slept alone after every encounter with those of the female persuasion. No one has ever stayed over and I certainly never considered it, but here I am now, seeing that it was right of me to wait on the right one.

Reyha.

She's the one. I've always known that, but I've never been with her until last night, yet here I am.

Stricken.

There's no other word for this feeling.

It's as horrific as it is wonderful.

Horrific because she hates me, and I've taken control of her and am forcing this relationship, for lack of a better word. I've always loved her, and my love has ruined everything since she didn't return those feelings.

My pride has gotten the better of me more times than I can count. I've killed people she loves to hurt her because she didn't love me as anything more than her friend. All my life I've known that she was meant to be mine, and she refused to acknowledge it. Refused to be with me. Refused this life that I now, after less than twenty-four hours, can't ever say goodbye to.

The sun is barely up yet I can see everything in all its perfection.

Lying here beside her in this cottage I conjured up. Our cottage. No one else has ever been here, and no one will ever be allowed in. This is our place. Her place. And it always will be.

Even when this is over. Even after both of us are dead.

She's lying on her side, facing away from me as I trail my fingers up and down her spine, feeling the warmth of her bare skin. This room is white, the color of purity. The walls, the furniture, the bedding, all of it. Nothing vulgar will ever touch this room. This is our place for as long as I can contain her and keep my dream alive.

There are dangers out there for both of us, but I can't make myself think about it right now. I've never known love, or bliss, till now. I've never known the woman beside me, not like this. I've known her as my friend in childhood and my adversary after that, until I tricked her, and now I'm the one who's trapped.

I can't let her go.

She rolls over to face me in this small bed we share, looking no worse for wear, but I can see the faraway look in her eyes. She's fighting against my spell. Her magic knows that something is wrong and is working to dispel me from her body and mind. I have to hold her every minute. I doubt I'll sleep much for fear of her breaking free of it.

"Where are we?" she asks as she moves close to me, making my heart beat faster with the excitement of her nearness.

"Home," I whisper as I lean in to kiss her good morning.

"I don't recognize it," she says, confused.

"I got it just for you. This is our first night here," I say, taking her hand in mine and lacing our fingers together as I pull it to my lips. I look into her eyes, loving her, wanting her, knowing I'm wronging her, but I'm in too deep now.

"I don't have any of my things," she says in a trance, looking right through me. Her state is a cross between drunkenness and amnesia.

"I've gotten you all new things," I say as I gesture around the room, opening the closet doors with a wave of my hand, showing all the beautiful clothes and shoes I've collected for her, hoping like hell that it pleases her.

"How did you do that?" she asks, bewildered by my magic.

Shit.

"It's nothing. Forget it happened," I say as I wave my hand over her face.

"Oh. Okay," she says as she leans up on her elbow and takes in her surroundings.

Her bare body is up against mine as we greet the morning, and I ache for all the mornings we should have spent like this. If she had accepted me. If she had loved me as she should have.

I reach out for her cheek and turn her face toward mine. "Good morning, my love," I say, feeling complete in my love for her.

"Yes. Good morning," she says. There's no love or emotion behind it. It's as if she's only half here.

I wish I could spell her into being in love with me, into feeling this divine utopia I'm experiencing. I would have loved her every day. I would have protected her and provided for her to her heart's content, if only.

If only she had wanted it from me.

"Darling," I whisper as I pull her mouth to mine, unable to bear the distance for another second.

She doesn't resist me, but she's not like she was last night. When she thought I was someone else. When she made passionate love to me under the stars as I wore the look of her true lover.

Jameson.

What a lucky bastard.

I kiss her deeply as I pull her body over on top of mine, running my hands through her hair, worshiping her like I've never worshiped anyone else in my life, wanting her to touch me like she did last night, needing her to accept me as she did before.

But I have none of that.

Her magic is trying to protect her, and it knows who I am and that she hates me. It's holding her back from me, making me want to scream and burn this place to the ground.

I roll us over, knowing she won't take control like she did last night, knowing that this is up to me. I kiss her mouth as my hands roam her body, working to excite her, hoping she'll respond as I want her to. I kiss her neck as she moans and runs her hands through my hair. I slip both hands under her ass and grip her tightly, whispering all my devotion into her ear, begging her to love me in return as I enter her again.

And I've never felt more in my life.

I take my time with her, kissing her as I make love to her slowly, deliberately, filling her with all that I have for her. I'm her slave; I'm whatever she wants me to be. And I'm rewarded with her gasping voice and her clutching hands, holding me as tightly as I hold her, telling me to keep going, to push deeper.

We both start to sweat as we pick up the pace and our desperation grows. I clutch at her breast as I look into her eyes and tell her all my secrets. That I've been lost without her. That my heart has been broken all this time. That I'm sorry for all the evil I've done to her. That I'm desperate for her forgiveness. She doesn't understand any of it and just looks back at me blankly as she has an orgasm that shakes the walls.

I follow suit, groaning out my pleasure and my guilt and every other thing I feel, holding her close as I savor every touch, every sound, every mind-blowing second.

And then it's over, and I can hardly look at her. I wish I felt nothing. My life was easier when I hated her.

I kiss her hard one more time before leaving our bed to shower. I make it quick and dress before she gets up, needing to get some air. I head downstairs and out the back door to find some peace. There are mountains and flowers as far as the eye can see.

I walk toward the stream that crosses over the backyard and sit on a large boulder, listening to the water splash as it hits the banks. I take a deep breath and let the mountain air cleanse me, watching the fish swim back and forth, feeling at ease as much as I can.

Until I hear the far-off booming of someone trying to break through the defenses I have in place to keep Reyha and myself hidden from the world.

2

VALA

He got her. How did this happen? And where did he take her? All I can picture is the smug look on Elias's face as he vanished with Reyha. He thinks he's won. And for the first time in my existence, I fear he may be right. I may have missed my window to get her back, and the thought fills me with dread. Where's Trixie? Can't she sense that something's wrong?

I race down the road to the neighbor's house and glide through the siding without disrupting a thing. The cat has a hissy fit. I fly over to it, my eyes glowing with fury as I let out a ghostly moan. It dashes under the couch and cowers.

I float up to Jameson's room and notice a dark wave of energy ebbing and flowing around his body, blanketing him in someone else's protection. He's sleeping soundly on the bed—too soundly. This slumber is magic induced.

Elias.

"*Expergiscere*," I command.

He doesn't stir. Barely even breathes.

"Wake up!" I yell, though he can't hear me.

I can't take it anymore. I've never felt so helpless. Even when I was dying, getting the life siphoned out of me by Elias, when all I could do was stare into his cold, menacing eyes, I had more control over the situation than I do now. I want to throw something across the room, but I'm not corporeal. I want to cry, but there are no tears to shed. I want to run and get help, but no one can hear or see me. Only Trixie can, and she's nowhere to be found.

Defeat, anger, fear, and pain boil up as I release a blood-curdling scream.

"What the hell?!" Jameson rolls off the bed in a panic and flips on the bedside lamp. He takes one look at me, and his eyes widen in horror.

"Who are you?" he demands.

"You can see me?" I ask, unable to shake the disbelief from my voice. "How?"

Without thinking, I float over to him. He stumbles backward.

"Don't be alarmed. My name is Vala, and I'm a friend of Reyha's. She sent me here to get you because she needs your help," I half-lie.

His stance relaxes ever so slightly at the mention of her name. "What's going on? Is she okay?"

"No, she's not. But there's a chance we can get her back."

"Get her back?"

I ignore him and glide over to his open closet and search for a bag. There's a green duffel resting on top of one of the shelves. I use my powers to fling it across the room and it lands at the foot of his bed.

"How did you do that?" he asks in a tone that could almost pass for interrogating.

"Pack a bag and get dressed. You're coming with me."

"Where?"

"I'll explain on the way."

"Not until you tell me how you just did that."

Sharing magical knowledge with any mortal is strictly forbidden. However, Jameson is going to see things on this journey that are inexplicable, inconceivable. Exposure is necessary. Besides, what is anyone going to do to me as punishment? I'm already dead.

"We need to leave now if we have any hope of finding Reyha before she gets killed," I explain, floating toward the door. "Are you coming or not?"

He takes a step back, his eyes the size of cauldrons. "What the hell are you?"

I vanish and reappear inches from his face, my irritation reaching new heights. "Snap out of it. I know this is all new and overwhelming, but I need you to keep it together until we find Reyha. After that, you're entitled to as many freak-outs as you'd like, but I don't have time to sit here and explain everything to you right now. Every second we waste is another second that Elias uses to get ahead."

"Who's Elias?"

He takes one look at my expression and holds up his palms in defense. "Okay, I get it. You'll explain on the way. Could you at least tell me where we're going so I can pack accordingly?"

"I don't know yet, so throw a little of everything in there."

"How long will we be gone?"

"However long it takes."

He nods and busies himself with packing. Once he's fully dressed, he slings his duffel over one shoulder and follows me out the door. He makes a pit stop in the kitchen to leave a note for Grandma, explaining that he's heading home for a few days but that he'll be back to visit soon.

It'll be more than a few days—*if* he comes back at all.

"Can't have her worrying and asking questions, you know?" he says rhetorically.

We exit through the back door.

Once we hit the street, I turn to face him. "We'll need to stop next door and grab a few things first. Potions and herbs, mainly. And a few amulets. You've already got a layer of protection thanks to Reyha's spell, but you'll need extra defenses."

"Spell? As in witchcraft?"

"You got it." I breeze past him and make my way for the Victorian, leaving him speechless behind me. "Legs, Jameson. Move them."

We raid Reyha's kitchen cabinets, and I tell Jameson to grab everything he can manage. He nabs an acidic concoction that scalds the flesh, an elixir that temporarily binds a witch's powers, two jars filled with healing remedies, a vial of poisonous moon berries, and a potion that replicates the ghosting power. If things get too dangerous, I can always use my magic to fling it at Jameson and lift him out of whatever hairy situation we're in. No idea where it'll land him; that's for him to figure out. He may not have powers at his disposal, but he's got a brain.

I tell him to grab two big handfuls of the black tourmaline to prevent attacks on our psyches. Elias is notorious for his head games. I came unprepared once and it cost me my life. I won't make the same mistake twice.

While Jameson bags up the crystals, I head to the living room and notice a faint glow coming from under a blanket on the floor. I use my powers to lift the fabric, and the entire room erupts in bright, burning light as the witch balls illuminate the space. I release my hold on the blanket and collect an empty orb for good measure.

"Here, pack this carefully," I say, floating into the kitchen and presenting the dazzling glass sphere in midair. Jameson hesitantly reaches out and grabs it.

"So bizarre," he mutters, shaking his head as he packs it up with care.

Finally, I lead Jameson out to the garden and supervise while he slips on a pair of gloves and carefully extracts the belladonna and the monkshood per my instructions. He wraps the roots in separate cloths and seals them up properly. Then he bends down and clips off some nettle and a pinch of vervain.

He transfers everything to the duffel, and before I can utter the word *abracadabra*, we're off to find Reyha—or whatever's left of her.

3

E L I A S

I approach the house as the booming gets louder and more frequent. I don't have any friends, so this is definitely a foe who's arrived. Am I to have so little time with Reyha?

I stand ready, hands at my sides though filled with enough magic to hopefully kill whoever it is that seeks to intrude. Then I see the glowing red eyes in the copse of trees, and I'm instantly angry.

"Why are you here?" I shout as I close the distance between us.

"Darling, is that any way to speak to me? After all I've done for you?" she asks as she takes her true form and rubs up against me. "Don't give it all to Reyha. You know how good I am."

"I don't owe you anything," I state as I push her away, disgusted.

"That's where you're wrong, champ. You owe me big. I've covered your tracks because they're all looking for you. Everyone knows what you've done and who you have. I think I deserve a little something for allowing you to keep her for the time being." She laughs as she looks around me and at the house Reyha and I are occupying.

I take her by the back of her hair and pull her face to within an inch of mine. "Go back to Dragan and leave me alone. Forget you were ever here and I might not hunt you down and kill you," I say as I shove her away, making her trip over her feet and fall against some rocks.

She flings a spell at me, and it knocks me backward, making my flesh sizzle as it burns holes in my shirt. I rip it off as it erupts into flames.

"You always had a pretty bod," she smirks, crossing her arms and looking me over.

"I said to go."

"Oh, I'll go, but I want my reward first—or my payment, however you want to look at it," she says as she sits on a squat boulder and leans over on her knees.

"Would you like me to cast you into a parallel realm? I could be rid of you for good that way and free to live as I see fit," I say as I whisper a few dark words in her direction, making her gag and gasp for the air she needs to live. I've turned it all to sulfur and she can't breathe, can't see much of anything though I can see her with perfect clarity. It's more in her mind than anything else. The sulfur is real; the blindness is not.

"Let me go!" she tries to scream, but it comes out as a begging pant more than a command.

"Then you will leave and let me be. I have what I want now, and I will certainly never desire you after this. I never want to see you again. Are we clear?"

"Elias, this is going to end badly for you. I was the last ally you had and you've ended that, so have fun staying ahead of them all. They want you and they want her, for different reasons, obviously, but with the two of you together, well, that's heavy motivation to find you and wreck you both. Don't say I didn't warn you," she says as she claps her hands together and shouts *discedite* to the sky. She's swept up in an angry cloud of swirling color one second, completely vanished in the next.

Thank the fates she's gone. Even when I was with her, I longed for her to shut up. Karina is a good match for Dragan, mostly because they are both as irritating as a flesh-eating rash.

I take a deep breath and sigh, now knowing that we're being sought. Of course. Why not let me have the one thing I've always wanted and forget I exist? Because I was supposed to kill her and take back her magic and her captives. The souls she has locked away in her witch balls belong to the Order and I am to recover them, though I'm not concerned with them at all these days.

I have more important things on my mind, and as I see Reyha appear on the back balcony with a cup of coffee, my heart skips a beat.

I run to the house and up the outside stairs to join her. When I emerge she startles, jumping to her feet, dropping the cup.

"It's okay, darling. It's just me," I say as I force a spell out of my hand to surround and confuse her. Her instincts are exceptional. They're still working, though I've hidden from her what her feelings mean.

"Right. Sorry," she says as she sits back down and looks out over the fields of flowers and swaying grasses. She looks like she belongs here.

"I'll get you another cup of coffee," I say as I step back into the house and to the kitchen, where I see she's been busy trying to remember.

She's dumped every bit of herbs and salts that were stocked on the shelves. She's mixed them all in a pot that would normally be used to cook pasta. I sigh as I cast them out of being and go for the coffee. One for her, and a large one for me. I have no idea how she takes it. I shout out to ask how she'd like it, and she tells me one sugar, two cream, and I add accordingly.

I walk back to join her and look out over the peace and beauty of this place and see the life I could've had, and it makes me angry again. I drink my coffee in sullen silence as she drinks hers oblivious to me in every way.

A twinge in my left temple tells me her magic is active, so I cover her in more of mine to try to crush it back. I wish I could remove all her magic from her being and live in peace.

And now it's time to drop my coffee cup. Why not? Why not take her magic? If I can find a way to do it, I can keep her. She wouldn't be strong enough to fight me, and she would become used to this beautiful life I'm providing.

When a witch is banished, there's a ceremony to wipe her powers clean. It's a well-guarded secret, but if I could find it, well, it could mean all the difference.

I feel better about my predicament and have a bit of hope for the future and for my chances to keep my love safely here with me as I begin to think out my plan to keep what I stole.

4

KARINA

I arrive back at the house only to be greeted by silence. Where is everybody? Did they all decide to take a vacation day while I got my ass handed to me for the third time in two weeks?

I need a drink.

I head to the kitchen and grab a glass of pinot gris to rid my mouth of the lingering sulfur taste. Paulina, our live-in chef and Elias's human host, must've taken the night off early. We've got to figure out what to do with her now that Elias is gone. There's no point in keeping her around anymore. She's a liability.

I make a mental note to tell her to move her stuff out in the morning, and then I'll wipe her memory of anything pertaining to me, Dragan, Elias, and this place. She'll go on to live a normal, happy, unremarkable human life, completely oblivious to all the magic that exists in this world. Elias always kills his hosts when he's finished with them, just like he did to Finn, but Paulina has served us well, and she deserves better than that. Like a happy ending, I'm gonna wrap this whole thing up nicely for her and stick a pretty, little bow on it.

Elias is lucky I didn't ruin his sham of a relationship right then and there when I had the chance. I could've given Reyha that little extra push of magic she needed to bring her will and cognizance to the forefront, but patience is a virtue, so they say. I must keep reminding myself of that on days like today when I'm sick of playing the dim-witted sex doll routine.

It's imperative that I keep Elias distracted. If he catches on to our plan, we're all doomed. Dragan and I have been ordered to execute Elias if he doesn't kill Reyha by tomorrow night. It's not a thought I relish, but the Midnight Order has set things in motion and there's no going back now. Once Elias realizes his mistake, it'll be too late.

I still haven't quite figured out what the Order wants with Reyha. Why go to all this trouble for one witch, especially one who doesn't pose any real threat to their establishment? Reyha is powerful, yes, but she keeps to herself. Although, something tells me that won't be the case for long.

"Dragan," I call out.

My lover appears before me in a cloud of smoke. He looks weary, his eyes sunken in and his face ashen. He lifts his chin, and a wave of relief washes over him when he sees me.

Then he collapses.

"Dragan!" I rush to his side to help him up, checking for any obvious injuries. "Here, let me mix you up one of my healing potions."

He brushes me off. "No need, my love. I'll be fine in a few hours."

"What happened? Did someone attack you?"

He slowly makes his way to the head of the dining table and sits down. I grab my glass of wine and hand it to him, sensing he needs it more than I do.

"Tell me everything," I demand.

He downs the wine in one go and lets out a heavy sigh. "I was searching for Beatrix's body out back when I got summoned for an impromptu meeting with the Midnight Order. They tore into me, hoping to dig up something on Elias's whereabouts. When I couldn't give them what they wanted, they drained me within an inch of my life. I'm amazed I had enough energy left to answer your call." He leans back against the chair and his whole body goes lax. "Did you get any closer to finding him?"

"He's hiding out in the Swiss Alps."

"Is Reyha with him?"

"Physically, yes. Mentally, no. He has her under some spell."

"Figures. It's the only way he can keep her," Dragan says.

"Maybe for now, but things are about to get spicy. The summer solstice is tomorrow, remember? Reyha's going to level up significantly. I don't think Elias has enough power to contain her within that house, let alone within her own mind."

"So what are you suggesting we do?"

"Nothing. We sit back and wait to see how this plays out. If by some miracle the two of them haven't slaughtered each other by tomorrow night, then we'll decide our next move."

"Sounds like a plan."

5

T R I X I E

Dark. Can't breathe. Can't move.

But I'm alive and that's where it's at. As long as I can hold on, I can get him back. As long as my magic holds out and I continue to draw on the strength from the solstice, I'm going to be fine. For now it feels like I'm stuck between life and death, but that will pass and I'll reclaim my place in the real world.

First things first. I need to break free of my magic. Elias surrounded me with his intent to kill me, but my covering is stronger than his spell. Once again the prick underestimated me, and it's the only reason I'm still alive.

I can only take short, shallow breaths. There's so much crushing pressure on me that it feels like a python is trying to squeeze the life out of me so he can eat me at his leisure. Elias is a fucking snake so that's a pretty fitting analogy, but when I get free I'm going to heal myself and kill the son of a bitch.

I can move only my little fingers, but they are enough to try to make my spell twist from protection to expulsion. I need to have my magic double back on his death curse and allow me to crawl free. It's going to be like peeling a banana.

With my arms pinned to my chest and my shallow breathing I whisper my counter curse to change my spell and inflict it on his. I tell my magic to open around my eyes to allow me to see where I am. Gaining about four inches of opening, the air feels good, even if it is smoky as fuck. I squeeze my eyes closed to keep the fumes from stinging them.

I roll to the left and look around as much as I can and see that I do seem to be alone. That's one in my favor. I feel my pinkies flex and pop as I will all my magic from them. I know this will be a slow process and I have to be patient. If any of Elias's curse touches me, it will kill me. I have to keep my magic between us.

The top opens around my head as if a flower is blooming at high speed, and as it reaches my neck, I see more of my environment and I remember. We burned the place down. All the way down. There's literally nothing left of the guest house but a pile of rocks and a few springs from the furniture. I keep my focus in spite of this and make my spell roll down my body and absorb what's left of his. I'm slowly becoming visible again. Why our spells smashing together made me invisible, I don't know, but I'm sure it worked in my favor. I'm stronger than Elias. I've always known it, but he's arrogant enough to think he got the best of me.

Finally my hands are free and I can take a full breath. I gasp and suck at the tarnished air, breathing in soot and oxygen at the same time, not caring that it stings my throat and makes me want a big bottle of Guinness to wash it down.

Once I'm free, I kick the last bit of the tight goo that was my salvation from my feet. I watch as it folds in over and over again, taking his pitiful curse in and squashing it into nothing. I lie on the ground and look up at the stars, grateful for the darkness, and roll over and dry heave my guts out—whether from anxiety or anger or the toxic nature of Elias's death curse, I don't know. I cough and choke and spit for what seems like an incredibly long time, but eventually I get my stomach under control and fight to stand on my weakened legs.

I need to eat and to dump every healing spell I can find at the house over myself. I need water to replenish and food for strength, but I won't be able to hold any of that in if I don't heal first.

My ribs are aching like hell from being all but smashed into my back as I held myself together. My head hurts, my eyes ache, my boobs feel like they've been trampled on…and those are the highlights.

I wonder about internal bleeding, and so I start my unsteady walk home. I put a word out to the universe to alert Reyha that I'm coming home in worse shape than I left, but the message keeps bouncing back to me as if it can't find her. It's probably just that I'm weak as a kitten and can't broadcast.

I walk on, knowing that deliverance is just across town. I keep to the shadows to make my way there, to the safety of my home and my friend. I know it's far and Elias might still be in the vicinity, but I keep putting one damaged foot in front of the other and encouraging myself that I'll be fine, that the injury done to me isn't irreparable, and that the damage to my organs isn't so bad that I won't make it.

My shuffling, pathetic walk has to look like something out of a zombie movie or skeletons hobbling along, but it's okay. I'm moving and that means I'm not dead yet. I need a lot of things to make me right again but I have access to all, including a bathtub to wash Elias off my body.

I'll not think on that.

I can't escape the thought of Finn, though. He's obviously dead. Elias used him to get to me and then he was rid of him. I wonder who he really was. I wonder when he stopped being Finn and Elias stepped in.

Elias is going to pay for Finn with his miserable life. I owe that to the man who I would've been happy to spend the rest of my life with. I owe Finn justice. No, I owe him devastating revenge. I owe him my worst. I owe Elias a slow, painful death.

I swear on what little bit of life I cling to right now that I'll honor Finn as is fitting for what he was robbed of. He was lovely and kind and handsome. He deserved better. I wrap my arms tighter around my body to comfort myself, knowing Finn is dead simply because Elias wanted to play with my mind and my heart.

But why would Elias come after me? Fuck me? Reyha's the one he wants.

A terrible tremor shoots through me as I pick up my sad pace to get home and see if it's even still there.

6

REYHA

Sunlight pours in through the window and I open my eyes.

Something's not right.

I sit up and gaze around the room. White curtains sway in the cool, gentle breeze. The air smells fresh and sweet, with subtle hints of Jasmine and Edelweiss, and when I glance out the window, I see snow-covered mountains. If I didn't know any better, I'd say this place is peaceful, serene—an idyllic little hideout. But it's a stark contrast from the conflict brewing inside me.

Where am I and how did I get here?

A pair of dark jeans and a gray sweater are strewn across the bed, and I look over to see that the pillow next to me still has a head imprint. There's a whiskey glass resting on the nightstand with a tiny bit of amber liquid left at the bottom. I reach out and grab the sweater, bringing it to my nose. Closing my eyes, I inhale the scent.

Suddenly, everything comes rushing back. It's as if someone has opened a door in a pitch-black room, allowing all the light in. Horrifying images replay in my mind, ones of Elias pretending to be Jameson, professing his love for me, running his hands all over me, thrusting inside of me….

I feel sick.

I drop the sweater like it's on fire. Before I have a single moment to process this mind-body assault, Elias appears in the doorway. I throw the duvet off me and scramble out of bed.

"What have you done?" I shout.

He takes a step toward me, and I use my powers to hurl the whiskey glass at his face. He dodges it in one smooth motion and the glass shatters against the wall.

"Please, darling, just calm down and listen," he pleads.

"Stay the hell away from me." I attempt to ghost out of here, but an unseen force prevents me from leaving. "Reverse the spells—now!"

"I'm afraid I can't do that. Like it or not, I'm your only way out. You can't escape this place, and even if you did, the Order would be waiting on the other side to kill us both. And I love you too much to allow that to happen."

"Bullshit. Drop the act and tell me what it is you really want."

"You," he says. The level of sincerity in his voice is alarming. It's as if he's actually convinced himself that he has a shot.

"You aren't capable of loving anyone other than yourself."

He shakes his head. "That's where you're wrong. You've changed me, Reyha. We're meant to be together. I understand you in a way that no one else does. Your desire to rule, even though you refuse to play the game like everyone else does, your thirst for vengeance, how you long to be loved and accepted—that's what makes us so compatible, so perfect for one another. Why can't you see that?"

"You've been holding me captive and violating me in every conceivable way for your own sick

37

fantasies. You killed Vala out of spite because you knew how much I loved her, and you've spent most of the last century hunting me down and trying to kill me. How could I *ever* love you? You are evil and soulless, and everything you touch is cursed!"

"Do you have any idea what I've done for you, for *us*? The sacrifices I've had to make to keep you alive have cost me everything. Stop being so unreasonable and think about what this could mean for us. Together, we could rule everything. Just give me a chance to make you happy and prove to you that I'm worthy of your love."

"I'd rather burn at the stake than spend one more second playing house with you."

The last hundred years have been exhausting, trying to outrun this man, too tired to confront him and fight another battle that only ends in bloodshed. Somewhere along the way, it just became easier to flee. That was then. Now, it's time to go all scorched earth on his ass.

I chant and the floor starts to ripple beneath Elias's feet. He backs up until he hits the wall and watches as the floorboards gradually sink. I summon every bit of strength and power I can muster to create a mystical gravity well in the center of the room. It takes an enormous amount of energy to spell this into existence, even with the solstice giving me a boost.

The bed, the nightstand, the bookshelves, and the dresser all start to drift toward the center of the room. Crystal vases and books topple over and tumble down the well.

"Reyha, don't do this. I'm begging you," he says. It's both a plea and a warning.

The curtain rod gets yanked from the window and goes sailing below, the fabric getting ripped to shreds. The bed and dresser go next, and soon everything else in the room follows except Elias and me. He presses his palm against the wall, chanting ferociously to anchor himself in place. I increase the pressure and he groans in agony, struggling to fight the intense pull. He doesn't dare try to ghost out of here now or his particles will be sucked into the well and trapped in a disassembled state.

Elias uses his free hand to conjure a giant tidal wave of sand and forces it to come crashing down over my head like a tsunami. My body collapses under the immense weight of it all. My spell is thrust into limbo, the pull of the gravity well easing up since I'm no longer chanting. I use my powers to blast out of this desert burial just about the time Elias releases his hold from the wall. He starts wading through the sand to get to me, being mindful to stick to the edges of the room. I scramble to my knees to resume the chant before it's too late. He dives across the room in a desperate attempt to stop me and is violently sucked down to the bottom of the well.

I abandon the spell and make a run for it before Elias can figure a way out. I race through the front door and down the stairs, the chilly mountain air a welcome reprieve. The long grass whips at my feet as I pick up the pace.

The farther I get from the cottage, the more tired I become. That spell took too much out of me. Combined with all of Elias's magical defenses buried around the property, it's a wonder I made it this far. As I'm forced to slow down, I look up and notice the faintest shimmer in the air. For a beat, I suspect my eyes are playing tricks on me. If it weren't for the solstice heightening my senses, I'd probably never see it. This is all part of Elias's cloaking, no doubt, designed to keep me hidden away from others and trapped.

I conjure a bright, burning ball of light and hurl it at the supposed-to-be-invisible forcefield. My magic makes contact and ripples against the shield. Once it settles, I notice there's a slight tear in the barrier. I stagger toward it, but before I can make any real headway, the gap closes.

And then it hits me.

I conjure up another ball of light, this one bigger and brighter. I launch it at the barrier, putting a greater dent in the shield's defense, buying me a little more time. I look over my shoulder and see one of Elias's curses closing in on me, hovering like a dark cloud. I turn around and chant as if my life depends on it. I know I won't be able to break through this magical shield on my own, but maybe I can send out a signal before the gap closes.

As I spin the spell, I begin to feel Elias's magic crawling over my skin. A shimmery wave ripples across the barrier as the forcefield starts to mend itself. I speed up to finish the chant before I run out of time and lose all sense of awareness. It's now or never. If I cannot beat Elias or break his hold now, I'm afraid I never will.

Confusion seeps into my consciousness, and I can feel my magic trying to fight it off like a deadly virus. I squeeze my eyes shut and hold on for as long as I can, refusing to give up the mental tug-of-war.

Please find me, Trixie.

Birds chirp. I open my eyes and gaze at the beautiful landscape. It's utterly breathtaking.

How did I get here?

I hear footsteps behind me. A moment later, strong arms wrap around my torso and a pair of soft lips find my ear. "Shh, it's all right, darling. You're safe now."

My mind is telling me to breathe a sigh of relief, to be grateful that whatever threat was here is now gone. But as this man kisses my temple, my gut tells me that something is off.

Though what, I don't know.

7

TRIXIE

I finally round the last corner on the last street that will take me home. I'm afraid to look, afraid to see what's happened to my house. I comfort myself with the idea that Reyha was ready to move anyway and that this wasn't going to be our home for much longer.

Still, I hope it's unmarred.

It's dark but I can just make out the roofline and that makes me breathe a sigh of relief. There's no scent of smoke or ash here so I'm going to guess that the house is in one piece.

It's harder to walk now; it's been getting more difficult with every move I've made, but I'm here. All the healing in the entire world is inside those grand doors.

By the time I get to the front steps, I'm crawling. I have no strength left, no pride, hardly any will. I feel myself slipping away to that place where I give in and never recover. I see peace and light and I know death will bring me those things, yet I fight against it all. Why? Why on earth do I bother? I could be free of all that I suffer if I just stopped moving and lie down on the porch.

But I know Reyha needs me and that she's just on the other side of this door. I drag my body to the door and knock weakly, hoping she'll hear it, hoping she's in the sitting room hiding out from the nice neighbor lady who loves to talk, or reading up on spells, or even sitting and being pissed at me for running off, waiting to yell and throw things at my head.

I will take her in whatever mood she's in as long as it means I'll live and be able to tell her I'm sorry for being such a moody bitch.

I knock again and nothing.

She's upstairs, of course. She couldn't be down here where I need her to be, where she could be useful.

I reach up and grip the knob as tightly as I can, getting it to turn bit by bit until I can squeeze it open and slither inside, dragging my legs now as they have stopped working altogether.

"Reyha," I call out in barely a whisper.

Nothing.

If she's in bed with that guy instead of saving my life, I'm gonna be pissed.

"Reyha," I say with a bit more oomph, and still not a sound.

Don't tell me she's not home. That'd be my luck.

The kitchen is closer than my room so I haul my busted-up body to the back of the house, knowing I can find something to heal me enough to make it up those stairs to my bedroom where everything I need to put myself back together is stored. I curse every inch of the way, being angry at Reyha and Jameson and Elias and the sun and the moon for the pain I'm in. It would suck to be a mortal girl and just have to heal the old-fashioned way. I don't want to lie around for weeks and wait as my system slowly builds me back up.

Something's wrong.

The kitchen is all but destroyed. The herbs are gone, the cabinets are bare, and every door is open. Someone was in a great hurry to take everything. I don't feel that this place was trashed or vandalized as much as I think someone moved through here very quickly, grabbing everything they thought they might need. Reyha would never do this. The house is protected against such an attack as this.

She's not here.

I struggle to find some bit of herb left that will get me up the stairs, my hands splayed out before me and working vigorously as if I'm panning for gold. I collect small amounts of ginger and shove them into my mouth, knowing if my injuries are holding any evil residue, this will expel it. What I really need is a handful of turmeric, but there's none to be found.

I pull myself up to the counter, to semi-standing, and think I feel a little better, though I might just be convincing myself for the sake of argument. Then I see my mother's amulet and I scramble for it, knocking the rest of the cups and vials over and to the floor as I fight to reach it and slip it over my neck, knowing she'll help me, knowing Momma would never let me die.

The amulet begins to glow, soft at first but then brighter and more powerful until I can't look at it any longer. And then, there's only a soft stream of light emitting from it, and then there's nothing.

I've decided to live. I'm healed of everything that's ever hurt me, and it's all due to the amulet and its power to become whatever force you need it to be. Momma was a clever witch, but this is the smartest thing she ever did. The amulet knows what I need because it holds one drop of my blood inside its sealed charms. That blood can communicate with my flowing blood and give me whatever my heart desires—to a point, that is.

Using it too much dwindles its power. This is the second time it's saved me, but it might not have a third time in it. I'm not going to push my luck there, but I put it in my pocket anyway. Then I tear through the house, shouting for my roommate, my sister witch, my best friend, and I'm met with only deafening silence.

I go to her room and bust through the door. She's not here, thank God. I thought I might find her dead body or a pile of sparkling dust that would tell me she'd been disintegrated or whatever.

I tear through the rest of the house, flipping over tables and chairs, making sure I see every single inch of this house before I go full panic mode.

But she's really not here. All of her clothes are here. Books, trinkets, shoes, toothpaste, everything she owns is here, but with the kitchen ransacked and the attack on me, this all reeks of one vile bastard.

Elias's dirty little fingerprints are all over this incident, one way or another. He couldn't have gotten in the house, no way. All the spells and stones are still in place, but he got to her somehow.

I dash to my room and begin to pack when I'm hit with a plea that throws me over the bed and into the wall, sending me to the floor in a shower of plaster and dust.

Please find me, Trixie.

I gather my senses and push my message out into the void, hoping she hears it.

I'm coming!

8

V A L A

Jameson and I have been traveling for twenty-six hours straight. After hopping a train in Bangor and transferring lines in Boston, we are entering the final stretch to Chicago, our destination a mere two hours away. Flying was too risky. The potions would never have cleared security. Knowing our luck, they would've been confiscated and Jameson would've been detained.

I had almost forgotten what it feels like to connect with another person—if we can even call it a connection. Jameson has been quiet for most of the trip, opting for sleep and a paperback over conversation.

I glance at the title resting on his lap: *Principles of Insect Morphology*.

What a page-turner.

Honestly, what does Reyha see in this guy?

The train slows, preparing for its next stop. Jameson's eyes open. He sits up and looks around, seemingly hopeful. Once he realizes where we are, his shoulders slump.

"Welcome back, pretty boy. Enjoy your beauty rest?"

"I told you I'm not speaking to you in public," he says under his breath, his eyes darting this way and that, making sure no one sees him talking to himself.

The train comes to a stop and the doors slide open. Several passengers grab their belongings and make their way to the front of the cabin. Some chubby guy lifts his bag and drops it on my seat while he waits for the line to get moving. The bag passes right through me.

Jameson's eyes widen.

"I know I'm mind-bogglingly sexy and all but quit staring. It's rude," I tell him.

"Yeah, the dead girl thing really does it for me," he retorts.

The man in line stares down at him like he's crazy, and Jameson sinks back into his seat, flushing with embarrassment. He watches as passengers exit one by one. Once the doors close, he looks back at me and lets out a heavy sigh.

"This is pointless. Can't you use your...*magic*...to get us to Reyha faster?" he asks, clearly still uncomfortable discussing the whole witchcraft thing.

"Contrary to popular belief, we do not fly around on broomsticks."

"I wasn't suggesting *that*. But you can move things with your mind, so why not your body? Can't you teleport us there?"

"I don't know where *there* is. Do you? Besides, it's not like you could hop on for a piggyback ride and go with me."

"Okay, well, what about using a spell to find her?"

"Gee, if only I had thought of that before we left," I reply, not even trying to hide my irritation. "I can't cast a locator spell without using some form of her DNA and a bunch of other ingredients we don't have, and even then, there's no guarantee that it would work. My powers are limited in this form. Hence why I need your help."

"How can *I* be useful in this situation?" he asks doubtfully.

Right now, I'm asking myself that exact same question. Maybe bringing Jameson along for the ride was a mistake. Maybe this was meant to be a solo mission and now I'm stuck carrying all this deadweight around (besides my own).

"For starters, you can talk to people. Haunting houses is fun and all, but it doesn't exactly come in handy when you're trying to get information out of people."

"And who are we trying to get information from?"

"There are several magical communities that can help us; you just have to know where to find them. Lucky for us, I have an old friend who owes me a favor. There's just one tiny glitch: I may need you to do all the talking when we get there."

"You're joking."

"Believe me, I'm as annoyed by that idea as you are. Most magic practitioners have heightened senses, which means they can see me. But lately there's been a shift. Certain humans who shouldn't be able to see me, can—" I say, eyeing Jameson, "—and some of those who are supposed to see me, can't anymore.

It's not happening all the time, just enough to throw me off. I have no idea which way it will go, so I need you to be prepared."

"What does this person do, exactly?"

"Asen has the gift of finding people. We're going to use his magic to figure out where Elias is hiding Reyha. It's not an exact science, but he'll be able to locate the general region where she's at."

"So we use this guy's powers to find Reyha and then what? That still doesn't get us to her, just near her."

"I'm hoping that once we get there, I'll be able to sense her magic. We can use that as a compass to guide us the rest of the way, unless of course Elias has shielded her from us. In that case, we'll use the witch ball to find them."

"Witch ball?"

"The glass ornament you packed. Those things detect, lure, and capture evil. If we get close enough to Elias, it'll glow like a freight train in the night."

Alarm washes over Jameson's features, and then I remember he saw me carrying one of those back at the house while it was alight.

"Relax, I'm not evil. Those things also happen to love ghosts for some reason," I explain.

"If the witch ball glows around you, how will we know if Elias is nearby?"

"You'll need to carry it so I can stay far enough behind to avoid triggering it."

"You're going to send the human in first?"

"Elias is already expecting me. He knows I saw him take Reyha, and he knows I'd do anything to get her back, but you...he'll never see that one coming."

"You're leaving a lot to chance, don't you think?"

"Rule number one when practicing witchcraft: trust your instincts. My instincts are telling me this is going to work."

He sits back and glances out the window, seemingly mulling over everything I've said. "So what does Elias want with Reyha?" he finally asks.

"It's hard to say at this point. The power struggle between those two goes back nearly 200 years. For a long time, he was in love with her, but the feeling was never mutual. Then he decided to go rogue, and he's been trying to kill her ever since. I'm assuming he didn't go through with it when he took her, otherwise why would I still be hanging around? I was brought back to watch over her, to be her guardian. If there was nothing left to protect..."

"Sounds like failure defines this guy."

"I wouldn't say that. He succeeded at killing me," I respond, my voice devoid of emotion.

Jameson has the decency to look remorseful. "Shit, I'm sorry."

"It's fine. I'm over it now. Don't get me wrong, I'd love to annihilate the bastard if given the opportunity, but I've long since accepted my fate."

"You said all this has been going on for nearly 200 years. How old is Reyha anyway?"

"Don't you know it's rude to ask a woman's age?"

He shoots me a look and I relent.

"She's just shy of two hundred."

Jameson shifts around in his seat like he's unsure how he feels about that news.

"Elias was there at the beginning when they were kids," I explain. "Trixie and I came along later."

"Trixie's a witch too?" Jameson asks, surprised.

"Everyone in Reyha's circle is magical. You're the exception, for reasons I don't understand."

He lets that one sit for a beat. "Don't take this the wrong way, but none of you look your age. Do you spell yourselves to stay young?"

"Some of us do, but that doesn't usually happen for a few hundred years. We have longer, enchanted lifespans, and we age much slower than humans. We're not immortal, though, as you can see," I say, gesturing to my own ethereal form.

"What about your powers? Are you born with them?"

"Yes, but there are limits to what we can do. Some of us can wield more magic than others, but the same rules apply to all of us. If we use too much magic, it starts to drain us, and then we have to replenish—either through potions, herbs, or spending time in nature, things like that."

"What happens if you drain all of your magic?" he asks.

"Then we're rendered defenseless, making us easy prey. Now then, are there any other burning questions you're dying to ask, or can we table this conversation for a bit?"

"Just one more: What's it like, being a spirit without a body?"

"It's lonely," I admit.

Jameson looks like he wants to say something but ultimately decides against it. We fall into a comfortable silence, and I'm grateful his curiosity seems to be satisfied for now. I need to brew some ideas on how we're going to help Reyha once we reach her. I wasn't joking; Elias has his coming, and we'll be there to deliver it sooner than he expects.

9

TRIXIE

I spell extra protection over the top of the house so I can sit and think and do my level best to figure this bullshit out.

Who the hell would trash our house? How is that even possible? This is a fortress, and we've worked hard to make it so. Someone got in and stole a ton of potions and wrecked what they couldn't take. It feels like vandalism, but there's something off about it.

Vandals would've probably taken the expensive things too. The silverware is worth a fortune and would be easy to steal, yet it was left. My mother's amulet too. That leads me to believe it was regular human type people who did this, but I'm still missing something.

Then it hits me. The only regular human I know is Jameson, yet he's welcomed here. He'd have no reason to damage things. But if he was compelled, if he or his grandmother were threatened, he'd do whatever he was told.

Elias got to him—that has to be it. Elias can't enter this house, but if he could put the screws to Jameson, if he was going to hurt or kill someone that boy loves, he'd do anything.

We all would.

But where is Jameson now? Would Elias take him or kill him? If he knows Jameson has been playing hide the salami with Reyha, then chances are good he's a dead man.

The more I talk to myself about what I think happened, the more wrong it all sounds. Pacing helps me think so walking it off will bring me some clarity. I let my mind go and stop trying to guide it where I think it needs to go, and I think of colors and clouds, of rain and of flowers, peaceful things that will distract me from trying to push. The universe knows what happened; she just needs to give it up.

As day turns to night, nothing has come, but I trust the process and keep strolling. I add a skip and a twirl to my path to try to pull some more calm to the forefront, but it's not working. I stop at the window and look out into the dimness of the evening, seeing my yard sparkle, my trees bend in the breeze, when I see something else—something I haven't seen in years, though I know instantly who it is and what I'm dealing with.

Red, glowing eyes looking all around, trying to hide in the neighbor's yard, unable to enter mine.

Karina. What a coincidence.

In an instant I dive through the window and hurl right to her skinny throat. "So it's *you?!*" I shout as we collide.

"Bitch, get off me!" she screams as we tumble and crash about.

"Where is she? What have you done?" I scream into her face as I crash her head into the large oak behind her.

"I killed her, you idiot," she says, laughing, wrapping her hands around my throat, pushing her thumbs in and trying to put my lights out.

However, her revelation has given me new strength. I grab two handfuls of her ratty hair and

61

jerk her head back so she can only look up. I pull until her hands are gone from my throat, and I hit her with a spell so hard I'm sure her ancestors felt it.

She careens out of control and down the sloping backyard of the folks next door, hitting every rock and stump. I'd like to continue to abuse her, but I need answers so I take off after her, running as fast as I can go without crashing into the solid objects on the way.

When she stops bouncing, she stands, shakily, blood running down her face as she opens her mouth to scream. I'm not close enough to stop her, which could be bad news for me, depending on the spell she's going to shout.

"Dragan!" is the curse to flow out of that big mouth of hers, and I know he will be joining us soon enough.

Good.

I hate him too. Let's get this over with once and for all.

10

E L I A S

I pace the room, marveling at how I managed to keep Reyha for another day. Now that the solstice has passed, the immediate threat is over. But if I don't fix this and soon, we'll always be running or fighting. And Reyha and I are tired of running and fighting. It's time we have our peace.

Wiping her magic from her body is the only way I'll be able to keep her and truly make her mine. She'll be responsive, present, full of life—not this mentally vacant doormat. Not this version that's trying to purge my magic from her system every waking and sleeping moment we share together.

To strip one's magic is almost unthinkable for our kind. We're born this way, and no matter which side you align to, all witches and warlocks are taught to revere magic. It's a sacred notion that's deeply ingrained in us, which is why we go to such lengths to protect it and conceal it from others. There are dozens of potions and spells that can temporarily bind a witch's powers, but erasing their essence entirely has only been done in the direst of situations. You'd have to misuse magic on a very large scale to warrant that kind of reaction.

Nothing would bring me greater joy than to perform that ceremony myself, but I don't have the necessary knowledge. It's a tricky thing, extracting powers. It takes extra skill not to kill the witch in the process. I'll need assistance, someone with access to ancient, hefty magics. Someone who's performed that ritual before.

The list is short.

My first thought is to enlist the help of the Midnight Order, but I've run out of favors with them. I bargained my way out of death once, and there's no chance they'll spare me a second time, especially given that I refuse to kill Reyha.

No, this one I must figure out on my own. If I step outside of this fortress and get caught, I'm a dead man. But I also can't risk summoning anyone to this location because then word will get out where I'm hiding. Worse, they'll be able to sense Reyha. I wish I could take her with me and keep an eye on her, but now that I have her all to myself, I'm not willing to jeopardize losing her in any way. She must remain here under my protection at all costs.

Suddenly a terrible crushing noise echoes throughout the cottage. I race into the kitchen, where I find Reyha grinding crystals in a blender. I reach over and yank the power cord from the socket. She stares up at me, confused.

"What am I doing here?" she asks for the hundredth time today.

"Shh, it's all right, darling. You head on upstairs and make yourself comfortable in bed. I'll fix you a cup of tea and be right up."

She nods and leaves the room. When she's out of earshot, I banish all the crystals, hiding them from her instincts. I don't know why I bother. She unknowingly continues to summon them back into the house and it's driving me nuts.

I grab a mug from the cupboard and fill it halfway with elderflower tea, and then I sprinkle some enchanted rosemary into the brew. I must be careful not to use too much of this or Reyha will slip into a coma.

I head for the bedroom, where I've conjured all new furniture to cover for the fact that she destroyed the other stuff. I'm still picking out the splinters from when I was trapped at the bottom of that gravity well. The pressure alone was unbearable. It's a wonder my eyeballs didn't get sucked into the back of my skull.

I sit on the edge of the bed and pass her the mug. "Here, drink this, my love."

She reaches for it without objection and takes a few sips. A couple minutes later, I notice her eyelids starting to get heavy. I grab the mug and set it on the nightstand and pull the white linens up to her chest, tucking her in safely. She falls into a deep sleep, one that should only last a day or two—just long enough for me to get what I need and then come right back.

I watch her for a few moments. She looks so peaceful, unlike when she was trying to kill me. I'll be so glad when those days are finally behind us.

I slip out of the room, not wanting to leave her but knowing I must. I do a thorough sweep of the property, tightening the wards and strengthening the forcefield, making sure to double-check every last barrier I've put in place to keep Reyha safe and throw others off our scent.

Here goes nothing....

11

T R I X I E

Before Dragan shows up I go to work on Karina.

Bitch.

I have her by the throat and am spelling as I look into her eyes to try to draw her memories. She answered too quickly when I asked *Where is she?* and *What did you do to her?* She said she killed her without a trace of confusion. Now that either means she really killed her, which I doubt, or she was just answering to answer.

Either way, I get the feeling she knows more than she should.

No way would she ever get the best of Reyha. No. Way. Reyha's too strong and too volatile to take shit from Karina. She'd look forward to the chance to rip her to shreds.

I feel the air tremor around us and I know Dragan has to be about to appear, unless it's Elias, or both of them. If all three of them unite here, I'll be seriously outclassed and they'll finish me off in short time.

I grip her throat harder, forcing her eyes to bulge so I can see deeper into her thoughts. I don't need to see her and Dragan screwing but it's in there. I see her admiring her tits in the mirror, shaving her legs, doing things to herself that I was happy not knowing, but to get to her memory of Reyha I have to delve in and take it all.

I get a brief glimpse of a house and Elias, some trees, and a heavy-duty dark spell rolling over everything, then nothing but a crack to the back of the head. Suddenly we've transported to a house, in Dragan's attempt to separate them from me and take them to safety.

I go flying, sprawling out on the floor as I hit the wall on the other side of the room.

I stand and run my hands over my clothes, wiping the last bit of his spell away.

"How did she get here?" Karina asks, her confusion thick as she tries to understand how I transported with them.

Dragan shakes his head at her, either meaning he doesn't know or they'll discuss it later.

"So, you lived? I wondered. You always were hard to kill," Dragan says as he throws an incendiary spell toward me. It grows as it hurtles across the room, but I hold up my hand and shut it right down, watching it splinter and wilt at my feet.

Karina is tossing her magic at me as he tries to distract me, to kill me, but little do they realize these things are only going to bring about their own demises.

I wave my hand over my face, protecting it from what's coming at me, knowing it will piss them off to see me use so little effort to deflect their pitiful sorcery attempts, knowing they will try to hit me harder, hit me with more, bring this house down around me without giving any thought to the fact that the protection spell I just waved over my own body has pulled the rest of their protections away.

I'm here, in their lair. I made it past the enchantments because the enchantments weren't looking for me. I was thought dead so, regardless of the fact that I live, they dropped me from the list of hostiles to keep out by their thoughts and intentions. Dead, I'm no threat.

And now I'm in charge.

I toss chairs and glass at both of them, throwing my hands up into the air as if I'm Moses parting the Red Sea, sending everything not nailed down at them, pinning them to the walls, making them cry out to each other to "do something!".

But there's nothing to do. They have done it to themselves.

I walk through the windstorm of debris, seeing the confusion on their faces as nothing touches me and nothing protects them. I can kill them with no effort, and they realize it.

"Are you going to give up what you know, or do I have to get rough with you?" I ask, looking from one to the other for any bit of a lie, for a shift in their eyes, for something to tell me they know, unquestioningly, what's happened to Reyha.

"What the fuck are you talking about, you simple slut?" Dragan shouts, but Karina says nothing. She breaks eye contact with me, as much as I can see she doesn't want to, but our physiology is stronger than our will sometimes.

"Wanna give it up, Karina?" I ask condescendingly, tossing more shards at Dragan, seeing him bleed heavier from cuts in a face that used to be really quite handsome, despite his shitty personality.

"I don't know anything about whatever the fuck you're asking," she shouts over the whirling wind, not too convincingly, I must say.

"Oh, I think you do. I saw enough of your memories to tell me you know what Elias did with Reyha," I say, bluffing a bit, hoping that Dragan will see the lie in her face and they will turn on each other.

He shifts his eyes to her, and he knows in an instant. He tries to break free, but I'm not having it. He calls out a word from our ancient language, and I hit him in the mouth with a coffee table before he can utter the other one.

These two words together could break me down. It could be effective, but it will take two years off his life to use it.

"Nice try. Don't make me pull out your vocal cords, because I would really love to. You try that spell again and I'll wreck you," I say, seeing the anger on his face as he contemplates his choices.

"Karina? I'll tell Elias I found him all by myself. You and Dragan can be free of him if you want that. I can kill him; you know I have it in me. Dragan? Get her to tell me what I want to know and this will all stop. I'll leave and you'll never see me again," I say, trying not to taunt, but wanting to gloat at the predicament they find themselves in.

No one speaks for some time, but eventually Dragan has had enough. The blood and pain have made him reasonable. "Karina, if you know something, tell her so we can be rid of them all."

"I don't know anything!" she shouts, completely telling on herself with the tone of her denial.

I let them argue while giving the storm I created in this grand room a little more power.

Dragan senses it and gives me the side-eye.

"Woman, I'm telling you right now, tell her what you know or be done with me forever. I'm finished with this," he says coldly, his voice dead and hard.

And it seems she believes he means it.

"Fine, you fucking bitch, have it your way. There's nothing left of her anyway but hey, if you want to mess with that, go right ahead. He has spelled them a house in the mountains where he's in control of everything. He'll keep fucking her until he's tired of her like he was tired of you, then it'll be on to the next whore who will spread her legs for him," she says, scowling.

"You mean like he left you?" I ask, knowing full well that she and Dragan decided to become exclusive but betting that she still desires Elias.

She's weak like that.

Her eyes glow red as she opens her mouth to trade another insult with me, but I seal that hole in her face with a wave of my hand and send these two disasters off to the farthest point from me on the planet. They are exactly on the other side of the world from the spot I stand on, and whether it's land or sea, well, that I don't know, but they're grown, they can take care of themselves.

She didn't give me much information, but it'll be enough. I saw enough in her memories to give me a direction, sort of. It's nothing I can't handle.

If he has her under his control like Karina said, I bet her magic is fighting him, trying to give her back control of her body and mind. He's planning to keep her as the little woman, the girl who will do what she's told and never have another opinion for the rest of his life. She'll have his children and warm his bed and never know it's not of her own choosing. She wants children, she wants a family and fulfillment, but this isn't that. This is slavery. This is Elias's desperation for a love he's chased all his life. This is him losing his hold on reality and thinking he can have her the way he wants her. But for her magic, he would win. Her magic loves her and takes care of her, even if she's unaware of it. It will be the only thing to keep her who she is.

Elias will know this, and my guess is he's going to get tired of fighting her magic, so he's going to try to hide it from her or take it away altogether.

This cannot happen.

I rocket from this evil place, knowing it's blocking my vibe and my ability to see clearly, and head back to the safety of my own home, needing to chill in the yard and sit at the altar, letting it cleanse me of my terror and take me to the calm that will allow me to find her.

I told her I was coming for her, and I never break my word.

12

V A L A

We arrive at Asen's condo.

"Stay here and wait for my signal," I tell Jameson.

He nods.

I float through the door and snoop around the apartment. The place is bright, spacious, and open. Floor-to-ceiling windows cover an entire wall, offering a breathtaking view of the Chicago skyline. The furniture is minimal yet functional. Every piece has a purpose, and there's not one ounce of clutter. Asen's motto has always been less is more, so it's comforting to know that after all these years, he's retained that part of himself.

Before me, I see a beautiful man with curly, dark hair sitting on the couch, eating a bowl of cereal. I smile fondly, thinking about the times we would stay up all night, confiding in one another and fantasizing about our futures. Or the times we'd prank each other to see who had the better grasp on magic as teenagers. He once spelled me bald right before I went on my first date, and I retaliated by cursing him with a bad case of crabs.

Nobody messes with my hair.

Through it all, Asen has been my rock. He is to me what Elias should've been to Reyha: a safe place to fall and a dear friend. And then my life was cut short, and I haven't seen him since.

Sensing my presence, Asen looks up and freezes mid-chew. His face turns ashen, like he's seen a ghost. He swallows his food and sets the bowl on the coffee table.

"Vala?" he whispers in disbelief. "Is it really you?"

He can see me; thank heavens.

"It's a lot to take in, I know."

"But…how? And when?"

"It's a long story. I wish I could stay here and tell you everything. Unfortunately, I don't have time to explain. I need to ask a favor of you. It's urgent."

"What's going on?" he asks, concerned.

"Try not to lose your shit, okay?" Without another word, I wave my hand and the door to the condo opens. A few seconds later, Jameson steps inside and scans the room. Asen's smile falters when he sees him. He jumps to his feet, his expression replaced with anger.

"A mortal? Have you lost your mind?"

"Last I checked, it was just my body," I reply.

"Both of you need to leave. Now."

"Asen, hear me out—"

"You know better than to show up like this. You're putting us all at risk just by bringing him here," he says.

"I don't have a choice. Reyha has gone missing, and we need to find her before it's too late."

"What happened?" he asks.

"Elias took her."

Asen's body radiates with tension at the mention of Elias's name. He hates that son of a bitch as much as Reyha and me, and I'm counting on that hatred to boil to the surface and inspire him to help us.

"Normally I'd do anything for you—you know that—but what you're asking for is forbidden."

"If there was any other way to find her on my own, I'd do it. But there's not. I need him, Asen. And dead or not, you owe me a favor."

He's quiet for a long moment, ruminating on my words. "If I agree to help you, the two of you must never breathe a word of this to anyone. Not even to Reyha. Can I trust you to keep quiet?"

"Of course," I insist.

Asen looks at Jameson.

"Your secret's safe with me," Jameson assures him.

"No one will know he was here," I say. "I wouldn't dream of putting you in that kind of danger."

"You already have," he replies.

Asen tears his gaze from mine and cups his hands together as if holding a small body of water. A subtle glow emits from his palms, and he stares into it like a crystal ball.

"What do you see?" I ask after a minute or two.

"Lots of snowy mountains and forests."

"That's way too broad. She could be anywhere," Jameson chimes in.

"Hang on a minute. I also see chalets. Maybe she's in France? Or Italy?"

"Okay, so likely somewhere in Europe, but that still doesn't narrow it down enough," Jameson replies.

Asen gives me an annoyed look. "Remind me again why you need him?"

"Because I can do things that Vala can't. And of the two of us, I'm the one who's putting my life on the line to find Reyha." Jameson drops the duffel to the floor and exhales his frustration, walking toward the view of the skyline. As he passes Asen, the glow in his palms intensifies.

"Stop moving," Asen orders.

Jameson pauses, and a look of confusion washes over his face. Asen swings his palms toward Jameson, and faint wisps begin to seep out of his chest.

"What's happening?" I ask.

"I'm not sure," Asen replies, shifting around uncomfortably.

We watch with rapt fascination as the wisps continue to exit Jameson's body and swirl around the glow in Asen's hands, like funnel clouds spinning in the sky. Asen harnesses the energy, trying to get a better read on Reyha's location.

"It feels like there's an invisible pull between us. My magic is tugging on him, drawing from his connection to her," he says.

"But that's not possible, is it? Magic can't draw from a human like that—magic latches onto other magic."

Then it dawns on me.

"It's her protection spell," I whisper. "She cast a protection spell on Jameson before she was taken. You're not pulling from Jameson, you're pulling from Reyha."

Suddenly, the glow in Asen's hands transforms into a thick, golden liquid and drips down between his palms. It gradually spreads over the hardwood floor, the beginnings of an outline forming right before our eyes.

"It's a map," Asen says in awe.

When the image is complete, a glowing orb drifts along the center of the map and then trails downward. It stops and floats in place, the light gently dimming and getting brighter again.

"It's a map of Europe," Jameson says. "But how do we know where she's at?"

"She's in Switzerland," Asen answers. "I don't know where exactly. It's hard to tell from this angle. But that's her essence radiating." He points to the pulsating glow. "I can feel it calling to me."

"It's hovering over the southern part of the country. We should start there," I say, looking at Jameson.

"That's a lot of ground to cover. What if we don't find her in time?"

"We will," I say, though my words lack conviction. "Asen, do you know of anyone who can get us there quickly? We're loaded with potions and herbs, so flying is out of the question."

"I think I can manage to conjure up some reliable transportation." Asen weaves a blanket of protection around Jameson, wrapping his arms and legs inside a cocoon of magic. By the time he's done, Jameson looks like a swaddled baby, with only his face poking out. It takes everything I have not to laugh.

"I think I'm beginning to understand what Reyha sees in you," I tease.

"This isn't funny," he says. "I feel claustrophobic. Let me out."

"No can do, pretty boy. We'd have trouble putting you back together again on the other side."

"The other side of what?"

Asen starts to chant. A moment later, a portal appears behind us.

Jameson awkwardly maneuvers himself to get a better view. "Oh, hell no. I'm not going through that thing."

"Oh, but you are," I insist, raising my hand.

"Wait!" he shouts.

I flick my wrist and his body goes sailing through the portal, mid-protest. "Safe travels, pretty boy." I use my powers to send the duffel through next. "Thanks again, Asen."

"Vala?"

I turn to face him.

"Please be careful. Losing your body is one thing, but if anything happened to your soul…"

I smile, appreciating his concern. "I'll be careful. Promise."

I float through the portal and appear on the other side, beating Jameson and the bag. A moment later, the duffel comes flying out. I hold up my hand to stop it in midair and gently lower it to the ground, out of the way.

A loud shriek resonates just before the portal spits out Jameson. He hits the ground with a *thud* and tumbles downhill, rolling right through me. His protection blanket unravels into fine, glittery dust and blows away in the wind. Jameson hops to his feet and stumbles around, clearly hit with a case of vertigo.

"Sit down and catch your breath," I say. "It'll subside in a minute or two."

"I'm never doing that again," he vows, dropping to his butt. "How did you beat me here, anyway? I went through the portal before you."

"One of the perks of not having a body—there's less of me to transport."

"Where's the bag?" he asks, looking around in a panic.

"Right up there." I point toward a patch of tall grass near the top of the hill. "I stopped it before it hit the ground, so we didn't lose the witch ball or any of the potions."

"Seriously? You couldn't have done that for me?"

"It was you or the bag," I lie.

He lays on his back and closes his eyes, taking deep breaths. While Jameson gathers his bearings, I survey the landscape, searching for anything out of the ordinary. I use my senses to try to home in on Reyha, but I can't detect her magic. We're either too far from where she's at, or Elias is cloaking her. Probably both.

Lush, green grasses cover the hilltops, swaying in the breeze and undulating like waves of the sea. Purple, pink, and white blooms are scattered throughout the fields. I imagine the tops of them brushing my legs as I glide through the meadow, their delicate petals tickling my skin. I try to remember how the grass would feel beneath my bare feet, and how that first breath of fresh mountain air would be crisp as it hit my lungs.

When I refocus, I see thick forests engulfing the foothills, the tree line sprawling for miles. Soaring above me are the majestic Alpine peaks, their tips dusted with snow. As I attempt to take in all the beauty and splendor, I can't help but feel insignificant compared to it all. Nature has a way of humbling me, and it's a beautiful reminder of why I loved being alive.

Far off in the distance, I notice a quaint little village, the dwellings huddled together as if competing for warmth. Parts of the mountains are scattered with houses, but they're few and far between. I'm betting Elias would choose an area that's secluded like that, somewhere with a lot of privacy and limited access to the outside world. He definitely wouldn't be a man-about-town.

"I think we should head that way." I gesture toward the mountains.

The elements have no effect on me, so this trek will be a breeze. Jameson, however, will struggle with all matter of things human—dehydration, fatigue, a time change, altitude changes, weather changes. I can tell he works out, so hopefully I don't have to worry about him falling behind, but a lot is being thrown at him in such a short span. I'm worried about his mental resilience. He's had virtually no time to prepare for anything or process this crazy whirlwind he's been thrown into. Honestly, I'm just waiting for him to crack.

Jameson trudges back up the hill and unzips the duffel. He fishes out a large hoodie, slipping it over his T-shirt, then he grabs his canister, unscrews the lid, and takes several gulps of water. "So what's the plan?" he asks, screwing the cap back on and tossing the canister into the bag. "I know you act on instinct, but I'm not going in there unprepared. I'm at a severe disadvantage, so catch me up to speed. What do I need to know to protect myself against this guy?"

Impressed by his confidence, I instruct him to open the duffel, and I give him a crash course in Potions 101, detailing what each one does and how he can use them against Elias. "Will you be able to remember all that?" I ask.

"If I can memorize over a hundred different types of bugs and name all their defenses, this will be a piece of cake," he assures.

"Excellent. Whatever you do, do not drop the witch ball. That is your lifeline. If you shatter that, the odds dramatically tip in Elias's favor. I think it's safe to assume that after what happened back there at Asen's, some of your protection from Reyha's spell is gone. I don't know how much of it was taken, but let's pretend you have none."

He nods. "What else?"

"You are responsible for the trinket the whole way. It may not seem like an important job, but right now that thing is our best shot at finding Reyha and protecting you. And as long as you keep that on you at all times, Elias won't come near you. If he does, his magic will get sucked inside the sphere and trapped. Don't let your guard down, though. Not even for a second. Elias can still cast and get into your head. That's where the black tourmaline comes in. Use that to fortify your mind. The potions are all fair game to use against him—save for the healing remedies and the ghosting vial. Those are for us in case of an emergency."

"What about you? What will you do once we get there?"

"I'm going to keep Elias busy so you can get Reyha out of there. If she's weak or wounded in any way, make her drink one of those healing vials. It'll fix her right up. Then I imagine she'll come stomping back to kick some ass."

He smiles at the thought, a sense of pride overcoming him. A part of me feels jealous. Once this is all over, if the two of them survive, Jameson will get to live out all his days with Reyha. They'll carve out a beautiful life together, and where will I fit into all that? Hopefully not confined to a front-row seat. I couldn't handle being subjected to that kind of torture. I love Reyha and I want her to be happy; I just don't want their romance to be broadcasted in front of me for years to come.

"We should get going," I say flatly. I gesture for him to go ahead of me so I can hang back far enough to avoid triggering the witch ball.

He grabs the glowing sphere and zips up the duffel and slings it over his shoulder. He takes a couple of steps, then stops and turns to look back at me. "Hey," he says softly, beckoning my full attention, "no matter what happens, I'll do everything in my power to help you kill Elias. He deserves to pay for what he's done…to both you and Reyha."

I'm unexpectedly moved by his comment. After decades of feeling alone and unseen, I can't deny how good it feels to be acknowledged and considered.

Jameson resumes his trek while I float here in silence, wrestling with the profound emotion I'm feeling.

13

R E Y H A

The fuck?

Why is the kitchen white?

Why is my head spinning?

I ask myself some more stupid questions before I get tired of having no answers. The last things I ask myself are: *How did I get here?* and *Where is here?*

I can only see a few feet in front of me, though it's bright in here. Too bright. I squint harder as I take steps forward, waiting to see something, hear something, anything, but there's only this void.

I find the box with all the cold stuff in it and I pull the door open, seeing there's a lot of food stacked all the way to the back. Packages say

"Reyha's favorite" and "special occasion" and "save for later."

Save what for later? I bet it's good, whatever it is, and I am pretty hungry. I leave the one that says "Reyha's favorite" for whoever that is.

I turn and walk away from the cold box and toward the counter that guy made coffee on the other day. He keeps telling me he loves me and wants us to be together, but I don't see it. I don't think he's my type, whoever he is.

My eye starts to twitch while the other one rolls up to the top of my head, and I bet I could see my brain if there was any light. I fall down on the tile floor, wondering why every fucking thing is white.

My kitchen isn't white. I hate white. My kitchen is bold and earthy.

My kitchen.

Do I have a kitchen? If I do that means I have a house and this isn't it. I don't belong here. As these thoughts come racing to the forefront, my eyes stop twisting and turning, allowing me to look straight ahead and see a set of windows showing me snow and mountains, blue sky and puffy little things floating around.

Clouds?

They're clouds and I should have known that. I should know who Reyha is since her name is on something in the refrigerator.

Refrigerator!

I remember, thank God.

I feel my mind start to race, and I try to pull myself up to at least standing with zero luck. I feel like someone hit fast-forward and my mind won't shut off until it shows me what I need to see, and that could take a while.

I think this is probably a good time for some coffee but there are only beans, nothing is ground. I can fix that. I hold my hand out and the blender comes to me, landing in my hand as if I ordered it. I don't know why I think this is an okay thing to happen. I should be freaking out at floating appliances, at my eyes taking turns rolling around in my head, at the fact that I don't know where I am.

I take the lid off the blender and grab a scoop of coffee beans to drop in when something that shouldn't be here catches my eye. A chunk of a shiny rock is wedged in the bottom of the blender. Why in the hell would that be there? Another odd thing I can't explain. I reach in and attempt to pull it out so I don't get it chopped up with my coffee, and I slash my finger open on the jagged blade, jerking my hand back and suddenly everything is clear.

"I'm Reyha!" I say with enough conviction to convince myself and anyone in the tri-state area, but looking out the window I'd say I'm nowhere near the US. This is foreign. This is Europe.

I swore I'd never come back yet here I sit, alone in a house that has no color or personality, in the middle of the country, whichever country this is, trying to make coffee that, truth be told, I'm not that fond of anymore.

Why am I making coffee? I'm still bleeding. I grab a towel and wrap my finger up tight. I pick up the bag of beans and read the front label, feeling the answer is coming, feeling that I'm going to understand any minute now, but the thought fades and I set the bag down and walk to another room, sensing there's something there for me.

More white. More blah and bland, more of nothing that seems to be me. Clearly, I'm a visitor here, but who the hell am I visiting? They aren't here, it seems. Maybe they had to work or ran to the store to get more ridiculously expensive coffee. Maybe they're off getting more labradorite.

Labradorite! Why do I know what that rock is?

What am I doing? Why am I just standing here?

My mouth goes dry and I hurry to the kitchen to get something to drink, feeling like I'm about to be turned inside out with the pressure coming from my throat, convincing me to hurry it up and drink some water.

I grab a glass and stick it under the faucet, flipping the cold side to *on* to fill my glass, but the water doesn't come out of the spout. It shoots straight up in the air, soaking the ceiling, the floor, and me as I fight to turn it off, but it's a no go.

I keep at it, trying to get the water to stop and not ruin whoever's house this is, but my hands keep slipping and my eyes are squeezed tightly shut to keep the water from hitting them. The water is blasting out now, probably tearing a hole in the ceiling, making tiles and chunks of wood fall all around me.

I step back, staggering, reaching out for something to hold on to but there's nothing. My hands come back empty—no curtain for me to grasp, no dining room chair, not even a friendly bit of countertop. I tumble, knowing my head is going to take the brunt of the damage, feeling sure that it will knock me out and leave me for dead in the flooding kitchen with the crumbling ceiling.

But I never hit the floor. The ceiling comes crashing down but doesn't touch me. There's a tornado bouncing off the cabinets, destroying everything but me. I swear there are shapes and patterns in the mess before me, but I can't tell what it's trying to say.

I sound crazy as shit right now. Shapes? Patterns? In the chaos? That's impossible, but as I say that, I see the shape of a Victorian house with shimmering light all around it. I see faces that I don't recognize even though I'm quite sure I should. A girl with braided hair. An incredibly good-looking dude that I hope isn't my brother.

Then, in the blink of an eye, Elias shows up and smashes everything into oblivion with a wave of his skeletal hand, jerking me to him as I hold my arms out in front, not wanting to go near him. I hate him. He's killed people I love thinking somehow it will make me love him finally if there's no one else for me to care about, as if the last one standing wins.

I raise my hands over my head to hit him with a curse I created in the event that I ever found myself in his presence, but before I get the last word out, he crashes a wave over my body, pinning me to the floor as he stands above me, rubbing herbs in his hands as they fall all over my face and chanting a counter curse that will send me into a blackness that will cause me to lose all the ground I gained today.

With my every last bit of energy I blast him into the wall behind him and wiggle out from under his curse. He's coming back and it's not going to be pretty.

I'm his hostage! His token!

He's kidnapped me and brought me here. It's why the kitchen is white and why everything else is so lackluster. This is his house and I'm living here.

No way. No way in hell am I with this monster. I would never in a million consent to be with him.

And there it is. What my power is trying to tell me.

My magic has been trying to wake me up to the reality that I'm stuck in—his reality where we play house and act like a happy couple. I'll kill myself before I'd ever touch him, but as this thought enters, a vision comes to the forefront that makes me lean over what's left of the sink and vomit every bit of anything I have in my stomach.

He spelled a curse to take my will. He's had sex with me. He disguised himself, and the best sex I ever had with Jameson was really with Elias.

He sees that I've figured it out. "Just slow down and listen to me," he says, his hands out in front of him as if he's trying to call a wild animal.

That's just what I am. I gather my magic and hit him with all I have and any other magic or force I can conjure from thin air. "You bastard!" I shout as I hit him over and over again, feeling powerful as I see his blood run down his nose and over his lips.

He always was a bleeder, even when we were kids he couldn't seem to keep the red stuff on the inside. Little wimp.

"I love you!" he shouts, and it just makes me angrier.

He runs at me and tosses a handful of dust in my face before I have the chance to protect myself and I fall backward, hitting my head on the floor, landing in all the debris, feeling it cut into my back and shoulders, and staring up at the second story through the hole where the ceiling used to be.

"I hate you," I whisper as I feel myself begin to disappear, never to remember this event, losing all the traction my power has given me, trying to help me escape, trying to save me. As my eyes begin to close and my fighting becomes a memory, I feel fire running up the inside of my left pinky. The pain is intense, but it makes me smile.

My magic has left a memory, a brand, something in my skin that will remind me later of what happened here. When I wake up, I'll see that and start to put it together quicker than I did today.

I taste ash and dirt as I fall away and I know he's using harsher, more dangerous magic to contain me.

I'll play it better next time and he won't see it coming.

14

E L I A S

Reyha got me good this time. As the blood drips down my face and splatters into the sink, I uncork one of Karina's leftover healing vials and toss it back, swallowing the mix in one gulp. A faint burn hits the back of my throat, letting me know the herbs are doing their job and putting me back to rights.

I attempt to summon Karina to tell her to whip up some more healing potions, but she ignores my call like I'm an ex she's avoiding at all costs. Since when does she not come running when I call?

I lean forward and watch in the mirror as the wounds close. I take several deep breaths, my body trembling with rage. The recent exchange with Reyha replays in my mind, and those last three words echo in my ears—*I hate you.* My hands grip the sides of the sink. In one swift motion, I rip the whole thing out and chuck it against the wall.

"Fucking bitch!" I roar.

Water sprays all over the floor, soaking my socks and shoes. Fuck it. The rest of the house is a disaster, may as well complete the look.

I walk into the kitchen and glance down at Reyha, her chest rising and falling slowly. She won't be waking anytime soon. Sleeping dust takes days to wear off, and when she finally does come to, she'll feel like she's experiencing the worst hangover of her life. Even thinking will hurt.

I stare up at the gigantic hole in the ceiling, occasional bits of dust raining down from the second story. It's all falling apart right before my eyes. How symbolic.

I ghost outside and pace the yard, trying to figure out my next play. The current situation with Reyha is unstainable. It's taking more effort than I anticipated to keep her under my control, and my patience is waning. I need her powers gone yesterday.

Thankfully, I found someone who can help with the ritual, but I was told to wait until the next full moon, which is twenty-one days away. Not a chance. I'm done waiting around, especially after this latest attack. There must be a way to speed up the timeline.

I think it's time to pay this sorcerer another visit. But first, I need to teach Reyha a lesson.

I take one final look at this cottage in all its glory, relishing all the hard work I put into making it shine. If Reyha can't learn to love me and accept me for who I am, then she'll know no peace, happiness, or solace. She'll be plunged into perpetual night, always yearning for the light. All the extravagant perks and simple comforts I've provided to keep her happy will be stripped away.

I channel all my rage and hate and unleash a curse so malevolent that it's likely this will come back to haunt me in another life. Darkness flows from my fingertips and descends upon the cottage. As the shadow spreads across the yard, the flowers wilt and die within seconds, and the grass morphs into a pool of toxic, bubbling sludge. The leaves on the trees curl up and crumble to ash, becoming nothing more than a whisper in the wind. All the pine needles turn brittle and fall around hollowed-out trunks.

I glance through the kitchen window and watch as the lights flicker and dim. The walls turn to black, the purity and levity stripped from the aesthetic. Every piece of wood rots to its core, causing bugs to seep through the baseboards. I close my eyes and visualize every room, repeating this process until the whole house moans in despair. I'll drain all the color and joy from Reyha's world without a second thought. Hell, if I could force the sun to stop shining, I'd take that from her too, but I'll have to settle for what I'm capable of manipulating.

Dozens of vines and tendrils pierce through the dirt and crawl up the sides of the cottage, covering all the windows and stealing Reyha's view to the outside world. I lock her in using every mystical means I can think of. She's now trapped inside this house indefinitely. No more morning strolls through the meadow, no more lying in the grass under the shade with a good book, no more dipping her feet in the fresh mountain streams, no more clean air, and no more sunlight or moonlight.

I wave my hand and a gust of wind sweeps the property, spelling an entirely different appearance to outsiders. To any random hiker who stumbles upon this cottage, it looks as beautiful and unsuspecting as any other abode. It's not until you cross the magical barrier that you're able to see this place for what it really is.

My mother always said the significance is in the subtleties, but I've never considered myself to be a subtle man. With me, it's all or nothing. Perhaps Reyha will finally come to appreciate all I've done for her now that she has nothing left to enjoy—no beauty, no comforts, no blissful illusions to keep her from realizing the sheer horror of her situation.

If she thought I was evil and soulless before, wait until she wakes up and sees her new surroundings. This lifeless shell of a home will be all she knows until I can erase her powers and make her mine. And by the time I'm through with her, she'll be so fucked up in the head she won't even know what dimension she's in anymore.

Paradise is gone. From here on out, it's nothing but purgatory.

15

T R I X I E

Karina is a liar.

I know that about her, but the thing she said about a house and mountains sounds like the truth. Too bad the dumb bitch didn't disclose what house and which mountains. That tells me that Reyha is utterly under his control. If she wasn't, if she knew what was going on, he'd have her spelled and chained in a dungeon with fire surrounding her and restraint charms on all sides. He'd have her so buried with magic that she'd never see the light of day again.

A house suggests he's trying to please her, trying to make her comfortable, happy even, but no way will that lie take shape if she is in any way aware of who has her.

I've seen so many things in my long life, and I know without a doubt that if she gets the chance to kill Elias, she'll do it. I believe he has her either confined or hypnotized under his considerable magical powers to believe she is with him by choice.

I can fight his magic and go toe-to-toe with him. I know I can, but he's not one to fight fair so I can't be either.

I've got to sucker punch him where it hurts, but what in the hell hurts Elias? What does he value enough to fight to keep it? Not Dragan, certainly not Karina. Himself only, maybe Reyha, but how do I use her against him? There's no wa—

Unless there is a way.

If he has her locked away, and if he thinks she's escaped, that will be the start of his meltdown.

A house in the mountains screams Switzerland, in my mind anyway.

And Bavaria.

And Tibet if we're going to run with this idea.

I have to find a fucking mountain that has a house. That's swell.

He wouldn't go to Vail or Vermont. He'd consider those places beneath him because they aren't *European.* He's such a snob. I don't even know that he's left the country except for the fact that he's ridiculously predictable.

So, what do I know about these places?

Precious little.

I leave the house and walk out to the altar in the backyard again to meditate on the where and how of my plan. I have to pack a bag full of Reyha's clothes and shoes, things that matter to her. I'll put the one picture I love of the two of us in my bra, close to my heart so my magic will know without a shadow of a doubt that Reyha is the direction it all needs to go. My heart is open to her because I love her. I would do anything for her. She knows that; her magic also knows that. It will recognize me. It'll help me. I know it's fighting to free her, that's the charm of our powers.

They are like living, breathing things. Our magic isn't cold and without form. It's warm and living. It's liquid as it flows through our bodies and waits for us to unleash it. We don't own it; it owns us. It cares for us, and when we aren't ourselves, the magic is still what it is.

An extension of us.

Her thoughts and feelings might be under attack, but it can't touch her magic. It's incorruptible. And it will recognize me.

I hold several crystals in my hands as I sit and cross my legs, preparing to project as I've never projected before. If I could ghost, that'd be more helpful, but I've never gotten the hang of it.

I roll the crystals in my hands as I clear my mind of everything but Elias, the generic mountains I need to locate, and Karina's fingerprints she left all over the scene since I know she's been there in the flesh. I can't trust myself to call out to Reyha and have Elias suspect or pick up on my vibe. He thinks he killed me and I don't know what's sweeter, taking Reyha back from him, or him seeing me alive and bringing about his destruction.

Getting her back is Number One on the list, but if I can fuck him up a little bit along the way, well, that will be a reward all its own.

I roll the crystals faster, gripping them, feeling the heat come off them as they grind against each other as well the skin of my hands. I need them to combust. I need them to blow up, I need smoke and brimstone, I need destruction, I need all the passion my magic can hold to find the way to him. To Elias.

I chant harder, telling my altar that I demand it to do its job and help me. I pull the roots of the trees out of the ground and weave them around the other trees, creating a stronghold. The wind blows and my hair is ratted and filled with grass and leaves and chunks of crystals as I put myself at the center of this out-of-control spell.

Not a spell; this is more. This is determination and magic and all the elements I can pull from the universe to cleave to me and the altar. I have to be more than I've ever been before and I cannot fail. There are no do-overs here.

When my body is lifted off the ground, I know we're almost there. The light inside my woven cocoon is brighter and whiter than anything I've ever seen. My magic has joined with the powers all around in nature and is doing my will.

And then I see her, and somehow she's not where I pictured her to be.

I see rot and darkness. I feel desperation and confusion. I smell that rich and terrible stench of death, and I don't know how mountains and Europe play into this terrifying sight, but they do.

Somehow.

I pull her emotions and hold them in my heart. She's upset and confused and lost and those feelings are more powerful than joy or love.

The fear makes her heart beat faster, so fast that it makes me feel light-headed. It makes me feel sick and dizzy, but that's good. I will be able to track her like this.

Whatever he's using to scare her is going to make it easier to find her.

What an asshole. He's too stupid to give it another thought. He's having such a good time torturing her that he's not paying attention to the outside elements, to the fact that someone, namely me, can find her like this.

He's so sure that I'm dead that he's not being cautious. And that will make it easier for me to find her and kill him.

16

E L I A S

I don't typically make house calls, but desperate times call for desperate measures.

"I'm not going to ask you again, Frederick. Move up the date of the ceremony."

"I already told you it can't be done."

"Magic always boasts alternatives, so there has to be one for this too."

"There isn't," he insists. "The presence of a full moon is critical to performing this ritual. Without harnessing that extra power, we don't stand a chance at pulling this off without killing her or ourselves."

"Then I suggest you find another way to steal her powers."

"You're not listening. There is no other way. Have you ever stopped to think that maybe there's a reason why ancient spells such as this are so well-guarded and hidden? If they were more accessible, everyone would go around stripping each other's powers, and then where would we be?"

"Nonsense. Most witches and warlocks wouldn't dream of stripping another's magic."

"Oh? Then what's your excuse?"

I clench my jaw. "I have my reasons."

"Don't we all," he says dryly. "That's my point. We're all brought up with a specific ideology and a set of principles that we're supposed to adhere to—a code of conduct, if you will—but most of us are quick to betray those beliefs and justify whatever actions we take in order to get what we want."

"Spare me the sanctimonious speech, Frederick. I don't care how you do it, just get it done."

"Forget it," he says, his tone resolute. "Go find someone else to perform the ritual. We're finished here."

"No, we aren't," I insist, taking a step toward him.

He waves his hand and my body goes flying through the wall at break-neck speed and lands in the kitchen. I rise to my feet and stare at him menacingly through the giant hole that's left behind, and then I ghost behind him, hitting him in the back of the head.

He spins around and makes a move to attack me, but I hold up my hand and chant before he can finish conjuring whatever was coming next. A red ring appears around his neck, and he begins to panic and struggle for air. I clench my fist, squeezing the mystical ring tighter until he flushes bright red.

"Move up the date," I tell him.

He shakes his head.

Suddenly, his wife enters the room. I grin, recognizing the wonderful opportunity I've just been given. No way can I resist pulling her into this mess. Frederick sees the look on my face and somehow manages to choke out a sentence.

"Alice, run!"

She races for the exit while I hold up my other hand and chant. A dark curse traps her in place and encircles her feet. It slithers up her body like a snake, then it enters her chest and wraps around her heart in a vise-like grip, just as I command it to. She gasps and clutches her chest, her eyes filled with fear.

"Apologies for the discomfort, love," I say. "I'm afraid it will only get worse from here."

I release my hold on Frederick and he doubles over, struggling to catch his breath.

"Let's try this again. You give me what I need, and once Reyha is free of her magic, I'll remove Alice's curse and let her live. You get the love of your life back, and I get mine. Fair is fair."

"What did you do to her?" Frederick demands.

"I put a ticking time bomb in her chest. For the next three days, her heart rate will continue to increase every hour on the hour until it beats so fast it explodes."

"You son of a bitch!"

"Don't worry, she's got time—just enough for you to get me what I need. Perhaps now that her life is on the line, you'll be more accommodating and find a way to speed up that timeline after all."

"And if I refuse?"

"Then you can look your wife straight in the eyes and explain why you chose to let her die."

He gives me a look of pure contempt, and I know if I hadn't just spelled myself that leverage, he'd vanquish me right here on the spot. But he needs me alive, just as much as I need him to come through for me.

"You have three days to pull this off. Understood? If you fail, she dies."

"Get the hell out of my house," he orders.

I crack a smile. "Let me know when you're ready to perform the ritual, and I'll summon you to the proper location."

I see myself out, leaving those two to scramble and come up with a solution to save her life. It doesn't matter anyway. Little do they know, in three days' time they'll both be dead.

17

LENA

"When are we to be done trifling with this incompetent fool?!" Izidoria shouts angrily, her bitterness and jealousy running down her face.

"We're nearly there," I say, wanting to hold off this conversation until the others arrive, but it doesn't look like I'm going to get my way.

"*Nearly there*?!" she shouts, irritating me with her insolence.

I raise my hand and hold it out in front of me in a very clear threat, showing her that I'm about to handle *her*. She takes her seat on the other side of the table from me. Her face is red; I can practically feel the heat radiating across the expanse.

"That's better," I say as she recognizes my power and the fact that I have one discourteous child to deal with already. I don't need her antics right now.

Lydia enters and nods to me in apology for being late and leaving me with her emotionally unstable sister.

I sigh in response, letting her know that I'm irritated with her, as well as with Izidoria. Izidoria because she's an idiot, albeit a powerful one, and Lydia because she left me alone with the overreacting idiot.

"Madam," she says as she sits at my left side.

"Lydia," I say in return.

She looks across the table at her sister, and I'm sure she asks herself the same question I've been asking since I met the two of them three hundred years ago. How on earth are they related?

I look diligently for reasons to exit her sister from the Order, but I have yet to find an offense bad enough to justify it. While I am the top power in the coven, I have to uphold standards and keep a mutiny at bay.

If anyone sees my actions as improper or unfounded, I could be cut out, but the fact that it's Izidoria, I might get a medal if I rid us of her troublemaking.

I would like very much to be done with her, truth be told, but until I find someone equally powerful to replace her, I'm stuck. The Midnight Order doesn't work if it's not five-sided. If I could recruit Beatrix, Izidoria would vanish, but until I can get her, this is the best I can do.

Oriana and Bree enter quickly, and we are five and ready to begin.

"Now that we're all here, to business," I say, standing, ready to present my case.

"Is it Elias again?" Bree asks, exhausted.

"Who else would it be?" Izidoria asks, heatedly.

I look her way, wishing I could fill her mouth with rocks or spiders to shut her up. "Elias is the only business we have as of today," I say, continuing my statement.

"He's not though. Reyha is the other matter. She's still breathing," Izidoria shouts, and I've had it.

I throw my arm straight out, away from my body and toward her, pinning her to her chair and stopping her breath for just a few seconds, trying to make my point.

"Are you finished?" I ask her.

She says nothing, but the color has left her face as she sees that I would truly like to kill her.

"As I was saying, Elias is the problem today, tomorrow, and always. He's been given chance after chance, and time and again the little fool has failed, and if not *failed* exactly, then he's certainly relying on his own opinion instead of doing the will of the Order. I, for one, am done. Officially, completely finished with this. I know his mother was loved by all and that's been the only thing that's kept him alive this long. We all know it's true; we can speak plainly at the table."

"So, what's going to happen?" Bree asks, her anticipation energy bouncing off the walls.

"We will, as we should have done years ago, go after him. In the process, we will take Reyha as well," I say, not wanting to do the dirty work myself but being left no choice.

"How do you feel about that?" Oriana asks, guardedly.

"Well, I'm not happy about it. She's been loose for far too long, and since she won't return, we will wash our hands of it and be done."

"And what of the witch balls she's holding? We need those. We need that power if we are to stay in control," Lydia reminds me, as if I needed it.

"That's something we have to plan for. I know what we *need* to do, but I don't necessarily *want* to do it. We have to dismantle her. Piece by piece until she's stripped down to nothing. That's the only way we have any semblance of a chance," I say, knowing we have our work cut out for us.

"What if Beatrix is still with her?" Bree asks.

"Beatrix will never be done with her, but as it is, as the elements tell it, Elias has separated Reyha from Beatrix for the moment, and this is the best chance we're ever going to get. We have to draw on the spirits to be shown the way. I know very little about the inner workings of that fool's mind, but if I had to guess—if I had to think it all out and try to figure it out based only on my knowledge of him—he's trying again, just once more, to get her to love him. She will never, he knows that, so he's got to try something new. He's got her under his control, no question because she'd turn him inside out and hang him in the town square with his innards dangling while he kicks and screams before he dies a horrible death," I say as Izidoria huffs, as if it's not possible.

"Only a fool would underestimate Reyha. Only a fool would spend her life being jealous of a witch who left the coven to get as far away from Elias as she could. You are a fool in every sense of the word, Izidoria. You are weak and stupid, and I'm so very tired of you," I say, saying things that we all know.

Izidoria wants Elias and blames the fact that he doesn't love her on Reyha.

"He was mine, at least he would've been if she hadn't lauded herself over him. I'm still not sure she didn't cast a spell to make him love her so she would always have a warlock to fall back on," she says, making my brain hurt with the illogical tripe she's spewing.

"I'm not having this discussion again. Ever. Shut up," Lydia says to her sister with fire in her eyes and revulsion dripping from her mouth.

Izidoria sits back, but she's not smart enough to just be quiet. She'll pipe up again with some other half-witted "theory" about why she can't have the one she wants.

"If Elias had killed her, like he was supposed to do, the witch balls would eventually deteriorate and the power would inevitably drift to us. Our magic would call it, seek it out, and absorb it, but he hasn't done that so *we* must, as distasteful as that is," Bree says with a sigh, dreading what must be done, hoping we can manage it.

"We have to get to Reyha before she is reunited with Beatrix. Together they'll be too strong for us. Beatrix and that temper of hers could likely take us out all on her own," Oriana adds.

"I realize you're afraid, I get it, but the five of us, focused and united, can handle this. I understand some of us have dwindling magic, I know—we all know—so let's work the problem. Let's work together to end Reyha and Elias, and perhaps if we are quiet about getting rid of Reyha, if Beatrix doesn't know it was us, she could be made to come back into the fold. Everything hinges on the way we handle things. That is paramount."

We all sit and plot and plan, and as shifty as it sounds, I will be able to hold control better if I can absorb the power from the witch balls, and perhaps take some of Reyha's on her way out.

18

JAMESON

W e've been hiking for hours. I keep my eyes glued to the rocky terrain and concentrate on moving forward, putting one foot in front of the other. When Vala told me to pack a little of everything, I should've been more thorough. I have plenty of warm clothes—I'm practically wearing them all right now—but no hiking boots or proper gear to make this trek more bearable. Some trail mix or granola bars would've been nice to have.

The climb is long and arduous, and the altitude is starting to kick my ass. My lungs are burning from the lack of oxygen, and I'm struggling to catch my breath. I keep telling myself to stay calm, resisting the urge to give in to my fear that I'll drop to my knees at any second and freeze to death like Jack Nicholson's character in *The Shining*. I'm lightheaded and dizzy and hungry and thirsty and exhausted and numb to the core. Every step feels heavier and more pronounced than the last, like twenty-pound weights are strapped to my ankles.

Too bad Vala is dead and can't feel any of this pain. She's really missing out. Then again, she'd probably spell every obstacle away and shower some more molecules into the atmosphere while she's at it. I don't even know if that's how her magic works, but the notion doesn't seem too far off.

I hate that she sees me as a weak link. I'm trying my hardest to add value and make myself useful and not burden her, yet here I am, completely out of breath.

I drop the duffel and rest my back against a large tree, sliding down its trunk until I collapse on the snowy ground. That's it; I'm done.

"We have to keep moving," Vala says once she catches up to me.

The witch ball shines around my neck. Carrying that thing in my hand was an accident waiting to happen. To fix that, I pulled the lace out of one of my spare shoes and strung it through the hole at the top of the sphere. Then I slipped the whole thing around my neck and triple knotted it.

"You go on ahead. I'm staying right here."

"Jameson, don't quit on me now. This isn't life or death."

"It is, and I choose death," I proclaim, resting the back of my head against the tree.

"I know it hurts, but I need you to push through the pain."

"That's all I've been doing for the last two hours and look at where it got me."

"Try harder."

"Are you deaf?!" I snap, done with it all. "Stop telling me to walk it off. We're not facing the same struggles. My body needs a break. I need rest and food and water. Walking it off is what got me into this mess."

I brace myself for a snide rebuttal, but she doesn't say a word. Instead, she glides over to me and holds my gaze. Tentatively, she reaches out and lets her hands hover over my chest as she whispers in what I assume is a foreign tongue.

A tickling sensation registers inside my chest, and then it spreads through my torso and down my legs. I'm grateful that I can actually feel something. As she continues to recite the spell, a sense of warmth envelops me. My muscles are still aching and burning, but I can feel the slightest bit of relief. It's just enough to take the edge off.

She stops chanting and leans back. "There. That should buy you some time."

"What did you just do?" I ask.

"I warmed you up and removed the numbing sensation from your body. It's a temporary fix, but it should last until we find you some shelter. There are several mountain huts scattered throughout the Alps. We just need to locate one before nightfall."

My shoulders relax, feeling like a weight has been lifted off me. "Thank you."

"No need to thank me. This is for my benefit, too. You're of no use to me if you're unconscious or dead," she says. "Now, open the duffel and search for the stinging nettle. It's a little bag of dark green, fine-toothed leaves. Eat a few of those, and they will replenish your energy and increase your circulation."

"What's the stinging part about?" I ask.

"The whole plant is covered in tiny barbs that sting and irritate the skin. You already have gloves on, so your hands will be fine."

I look at her like she's crazy. "I'm less concerned about my skin and far more worried about the inside of my mouth and the back of my throat—not to mention the rest of me."

"There may be a few unpleasant side effects, but the benefits far outweigh the discomfort. You need to trust me on this one. Humans eat this stuff all the time. They brew it in their teas, add it to their pastas and soups—"

"Yeah, but do people ingest it raw and live to tell about it?"

"Well, there was this one time…" she says, trying to cut the tension.

I'm not amused.

She drops the humor and gives it to me straight. "It's an acquired taste, but yes, some people eat it raw. You may be walking away with an upset stomach, but you'll be walking, and that's the point."

I unzip the duffel and search around. After a minute or so, I hold up the plastic bag and she nods, confirming it's the correct plant. I open the seal and take a whiff, still unsure.

"Nettle has such a wonderful, earthy scent. It's almost calming, don't you agree?"

"Sure, we'll go with that."

"Roll the leaves into a tight ball and squeeze them before you eat them. That will help break down the fine hairs."

I nod and pluck the first one out of the bag, rolling it between my fingers. Once I get a few of them down the hatch, I relax a bit.

"See? That wasn't so bad," she says.

"Let's see what happens to me over the next hour."

She lets out a laugh and my eyes find hers.

"I'm sorry for losing it on you earlier."

"Apology accepted. Now get your ass up and walk it off."

A couple hours later, it's starting to get dark out. The temps have dropped from freezing to arctic. Every time the wind whips, it bites my flesh. Every breath stings my lungs, as if dozens of needle-like icicles are piercing the tissue.

I stop hiking and gaze out over the horizon, looking at our options below—it's slim pickings. Then I notice a single cabin and a faint glow emanating from an open fire. It's practically beckoning me to it.

"That might be our best bet," I say, pointing to the tiny structure. "We should go check it out."

"Good eye," Vala replies. "Let's go."

As we get closer to the cabin, I stow the witch ball in the duffel bag. No need to draw unwanted attention. From the outside, the place looks small and warm and cozy. Several picnic tables are lined up along the deck, inspiring confidence that this place is meant for travelers passing through, and there's a wood-fired hot tub at the base of the cabin.

I walk up to the front door and knock, though the gesture seems pointless. Vala floats right on through. I tentatively open the door and step inside, looking around. There's a kitchen and a communal bathroom right near the entryway, and as I make my way farther in, I see the bedrooms. They remind me of my college dorm at UMaine, bunk beds lining the walls.

Suddenly, a petite, middle-aged woman walks up and introduces herself. Claudia has a thick accent, but her English is excellent. She tells me that she and her family run the place, and that she could tell just by looking at me that I'm an American. Unsure how to take that, I let out a short, awkward laugh and tell her I'm looking for a place to stay for the night. She informs me there are two beds available.

"I'll take one," I say, and she asks for payment upfront.

I slip my gloves off and fish my wallet out of my pocket.

"Do you guys take credit cards?"

"We do not," she says.

I have zero cash of any kind, so that won't work. I pull out my phone and turn it on. I've had it off since we got here, trying to conserve battery. I stare at the screen and frown. No service. Can't say I'm surprised.

"What's the Wi-Fi password here?" I ask.

"There is no internet."

"Is there an ATM nearby?"

"Unfortunately, the closest one is about six kilometers from here."

"Excuse me?" a young woman says from behind us. "I'll pay for his stay."

I turn around and nearly get the wind knocked out of me again, but in a good way this time. This woman is next-level attractive. She's so beautiful that it hurts to look at her, and I'm instantly reminded of the very first time I laid eyes on Reyha.

She holds my gaze and gives me a slow, steady smile.

"That's not necessary," I tell her. "But thank you for the offer…" I trail off, hoping she'll fill in the blank.

"Emma," she says, handing Claudia sixty francs, "and I insist."

That covers a place to sleep for the night and breakfast tomorrow morning. I nearly weep at the thought.

"Nice to meet you, Emma." I stick out my hand. Her soft palm slides against mine, and she gives it a good shake.

"Pleasure's all mine…"

"Jameson," I answer.

There's a brief pause, and Claudia takes the opportunity to jump in and give me a rundown of where everything's located. She tells us to let her know if we need anything, and then she excuses herself. Her cheeky smile doesn't go unnoticed.

I turn my attention back to Emma. "At least give me your email address so I can pay you back once I have service again."

"How about you give me your number instead?" she flirts.

If I weren't already taken, I would do just that. I politely decline and tell her that I have a girlfriend. A brief flash of disappointment hits her eyes, but she recovers like a pro. After a little persuasion, I finally convince her to give me her email address. I promise to pay her back in full for her kindness.

"Well, I hope you enjoy your trip," she says.

"Same to you. And thank you again. You saved me tonight."

She gives me one last smile—this one more friendly than flirty—before she walks off.

"You should've introduced me," Vala jokes over my shoulder. "I'd like to show her a good time and ruin her for all men."

"I didn't realize you swung that way," I say under my breath, walking away from the crowd so I can engage in conversation without looking like a paranoid schizo.

"Oh, I swing all kinds of ways, pretty boy. Funnily enough, you and I seem to have the same taste in women."

"Do we now?" I say dryly.

"We sure do—just ask your girlfriend."

I stop dead in my tracks. *Wait, what?*

"You're kidding," I say, somewhat in shock. "When were you going to tell me?"

She shrugs. "I wasn't."

Before I can stop myself, I ask, "How long ago?"

"Relax, it's been eons. You weren't even born yet."

I breathe a sigh of relief. Ancient history, I can handle. Recent history, not so much.

"What was she like back then?"

Vala smiles, thinking back to those days. "Softer. Time has made her harder—stronger and wiser, too, but harder. She used to be so spontaneous and wild. That carefree spirit of hers was the thing that attracted me to her in the first place. She was always chasing her desires, and she radiated warmth and beauty like sunlight. Everywhere we went, people gravitated toward her. It made me jealous at first, to watch her have that effect on others, but then I grew to love her for it. It's hard to imagine now because she's so careful and guarded and restrained, but she was completely uninhibited back then. Part of it was the fiery impulses of youth, but mostly it was because she hadn't been betrayed by anyone yet. She didn't have a reason to withhold pieces of herself from other people. I wish she could rediscover that part of herself. Heaven knows it wouldn't kill her to let her hair down one in a while."

"Why not tell her that when you see her again?" I suggest.

"Oh, she can't see or hear me. It's woven in as part of the spell that brought me back—all designed to help her to move on. Apparently, seeing your dead girlfriend everyday interrupts the healing process."

"And you don't want her to move on?" I ask, being careful not to sound accusatory. I want her to recognize I'm coming from a place of understanding, not a place of judgment.

"Things feel unfinished between us. I never got a chance to say goodbye. I would've done things differently had I known that was going to be the last time she'd ever see me again. That among other things has made this whole guardianship role feel like a punishment. I love and miss her so much, but I'm not meant to be a part of this world anymore. My time here was finished. Watching Reyha move on with someone else and be happy and live her life while I'm stuck here in limbo, forced to view it all from the sidelines in this reduced form, is not exactly what I had envisioned for the afterlife. So, in essence, it's not that I don't want her to move on, it's that I would like to move on and be happy too, in whatever form that looks like for me."

"Makes sense. If you had your way, what would that next phase look like?"

"I'd always imagined that my spirit would dissolve into millions of glittery, shimmery particles and float up into the night sky, allowing me to take my original form in the cosmos. Ashes to ashes, stardust to stardust. No pain, no shame, no regret or guilt, just a quiet, beautiful, peace-filled existence."

I smile. "I hope you get your wish someday."

"Me too. Now go get some sleep," she says. "I like you better when you're not asking so many damn questions."

I laugh. "I'll try my best."

We reach my room and I bid Vala a goodnight, eager to turn in and get some rest.

As I lay under the covers and stare up at the ceiling, my mind drifts to Reyha. I think about all I've learned over the last couple of days—details of Reyha's past, her complicated relationships with Vala and Elias, the existence of witchcraft. I need to see her again. I need to know she's okay. I need to hold her in my arms and comfort her after everything she's been through. And when she's ready, I need her to open up and explain this all to me.

19

TRIXIE

I wake up in the middle of the yard with people leaning over me, looking at me and wondering what in the hell I'm doing here, mostly naked and covered in leaves and ash. They're murmuring things like *Is she dead?* and *Where did the explosion come from?*

Seems my chanting at the altar didn't go unseen.

I shift to sit up and the crowd gasps and moves back, looking interested to say the least, terrified if I look close enough.

"Whew. Wow, that packed a punch, didn't it?" I ask as I sit up and brush off my hands and pull what's left of my top up to where it belongs. No one speaks and I'm grateful for that. I get to my feet and walk to the house, stepping on the crystals I smashed to bits, finding I've got a bit of a limp and a killer headache. I could expect nothing less.

My spell took everything from me and then borrowed against the power I will need to get back to normal. I'm gonna be weak for a while, and that makes me an easy target.

Must get inside.

I feel eyes on me and I know they're getting close so I limp and stumble faster, with less and less grace all the time, trying to get to the safety of the house before I'm snatched up and imprisoned or killed or whatever other torture awaits.

I pull my ass up the stairs by the handrail, dragging my heavy legs behind me. I get to my feet to step to the door, grabbing it quickly and swinging it open hard, throwing myself inside and on to the floor.

The door slams shut behind me, a little harder than it should have, and I am comforted by the fact that I knew something was there. All my senses are still intact. My aching head and weakened body have still been doing their jobs.

I lie on my back, satisfied that I'm untouchable here, inside the fortress we made. And my heart begins to hurt. The rafters start to squeak and shift, and I feel a deep sigh run through the house. I know that feeling. I know that sound, and it's agonizing.

The house misses her. It's more than a house. It's a living, breathing extension of us and it knows we are both struggling.

"It's gonna be okay, ol' girl. You know I'm good for it," I say as I pat the floor beside me and try to reassure her that we will all be reunited again.

The chandelier high above me gives a little tingling noise, and I know the magic surrounding our house understands.

I wink back at the chandelier and feel we're gonna be just fine. Rolling over, I work to stand when I hear a soft rapping at the door I just entered. I freeze. I thought everyone had probably left the yard when I came in.

I know nothing can hurt me here but still, I walk with caution. What I see hits me straight in the chest, and I know instantly that I'm in trouble, but not the kind I'm used to. No. The kind of trickery Elias used against me. The kind that got me into bed with him. But this time it's not a ruse. I know who this is because I put my hopes and dreams out into the universe, and she came through.

I open the door with a stupid smile on my stupid face that not even Elias could take away from me. "Well, there you are," I say as I look into those beautiful eyes and think that I could die right now and not have much to regret.

He's here. The man of my dreams. My perfect match, the one I wear charms in my hair for, the one I've prayed for, the one who will love me as I love him.

I know everything but his name.

"I'm Donovan," he says as he smiles and heaves a sigh of relief.

I sigh too and put my hand out to shake his and give some sort of official hello, but he takes my hand and kisses it, running his thumb over the little veins in the back of my hand.

"I've been looking for you and here you are," he says, stepping closer.

"Here I am," I whisper as I close my eyes and thank God and the universe, my magic, my lucky stars, and the rabbit's foot I keep in a drawer in my room for seeing it through, for bringing me my heart's desire.

"Can I come in?" he asks.

"Sure can. It's a bit of a mess, I don't know how to explain what's going on in terms you'd accept. I don't want you running out the door thinking I'm crazy."

"I don't need any answers you aren't ready to give," he says, leaning forward to rest his head against mine and I feel seen and understood for maybe the first time in my life.

"That's good to know. Someday, when we know each other better, I will spill it all," I say, directing him to come upstairs to help me get ready to go.

I stop midway up to the second floor.

"Will you stay here? In the safety of the house until I return?" I ask, knowing he'll say yes.

He agrees to wait and we hurry to my room to get me on my way.

While helping me pack my clothes and a variety of odd bottles and materials he asks nothing about all the weird shit he sees. I have the flowers growing in the closet that I use for my beauty and healthcare line with pure sunlight pouring from a spout of my own magical creation, and he acts like it's as normal as mosquitoes in July.

He's incredible. He's the whole package and I feel as if I'm the luckiest, most blessed girl ever born. I want to stay and hold hands and look into his eyes forever, but today isn't that day.

I ask him to grab the other bag from the closet where the sunlight is of a different potency, and he does. Without a questioning look, without fear. He's here for me, and all the weird things that surround me don't seem to bother him a bit.

He really is here for me.

We keep looking, glancing back and forth at each other while we pack. He's adorable and sweet, and I'm so blown away that my spell worked so well. I didn't create him and I didn't fool him. My magic was sent out into the world and brought forth the one who was meant for me, though I didn't know how or where to find him on my own.

I listed the things I wanted, wore charms to keep things fresh in my thoughts and current with my magic, but could never make a spell precise enough to encapsulate all the wonderful things he's going to show me. I have things I want as a rule, but all people are so deep and complex that there's no way I could ever come close to listing all the marvelous things about him.

146

I wanted someone who would be kind to me and nice to look at. I wanted someone who would be loyal and smart, but those are fairly basic. What about hobbies? What if he's someone who fishes every weekend? What if he sings and writes poetry? What if he's good at card games? These are things I could never hope to ask for.

Those are the small things that I would be surprised by. To tell you the truth, I hope he's got plans and desires for the future, and I hope that he wants to include me. I haven't fished since I was a little witch. My singing sucks. I love to play cards but don't have anyone who can beat me.

I hope he's better at things than I am. Not better at everything, but better at something. I hope he challenges me in ways I've never thought of. I hope his conversation skills are on point and that he gets me to give new things a chance.

And the last thing on my mind is sex. He's luscious, make no mistake, but I want the things that sex with some guy can't give me.

A real, true intimacy.

Sex is intimate, sure, but that is only part of the connection. Only half of what I want from him. I want to sit on the porch and watch the sun rise, holding hands and wrapped in blankets when it's chilly. I want to be able to tell him about my past life and have him believe me and not find it scary that I've been alive for a long time. I want to know the things he likes. I want to fight occasionally and make up a couple of hours later.

I want vows. I want some pretty children. I want it all.

These thoughts make me warm, and I can't hide the smile from my face. I look over and he's watching me with a look of sincerity.

"I want it all, too," he says, smiling and nodding.

And I'm mortified.

"You have abilities?" I ask, shocked that I didn't sense it before.

"No, not like yours, but I'm intuitive. I can usually read the room. I can sense what people are feeling, and you and I are on the same page," he says and looks down at the bed where he's packing the last remnants of my top dresser drawer, a dash of a smile on his lovely face.

Once all is packed I hug him tightly, wrapping my arms around his neck as he hugs me around my waist and lifts me, his face buried in my hair as we whisper our goodbyes. He tells me to be safe on whatever mission I'm on. I ask him to stay in the house and not to leave for any reason. I tell him I'm not going to have much luck on my quest if I'm worried someone is going to grab him and force me to make a choice.

"Is there food in the house?" he asks.

"Yeah, tons," I say.

"Okay then, I have no reason to venture out. I'll stay in the fortress until you come back," he says, kissing my cheek.

We untangle from each other and I walk to the window, focusing on what I want to find, what I want to feel, and for any curious bit of magic on the air tonight to clue me in to what part of the world I need to try first.

I look back for just a second to see him standing in the middle of my room, arms crossed over his chest, a smile on his face, and I am gone in a flash of light, off to find that silly friend of mine so I can hurry back to my man and start my life with him.

Donovan…something. I didn't even think to ask the rest of his name. I didn't need to.

20

KARINA

That stupid little twat's spell dropped us in the middle of the ocean, right near Australia. Joke's on her. I was dying for a good swim.

Now we're living it up in the Land Down Under. Dragan and I have opted to stay here for the time being. We're sick of the drama, and we keep getting pulled into it from all sides. While those imbeciles are busy fighting each other, I'm going to continue to lay topless on this beach and enjoy cocktails with my man. I've gotten laid more times than I can count since we got here, and boy do I feel better. Sex and sun do a girl good.

We may as well enjoy the peace and quiet while we can. It's only a matter of time before the Midnight Order summons us again. Although, I suspect right now they're far too busy trying to find Elias and Reyha. It'll be a while before they come a-knocking.

Fine by me.

"You know, of all the places Beatrix could've sent us to, this sure isn't bad," Dragan says, removing his drink umbrella and taking a sip of his piña colada. "Maybe we should let her kick our asses more often."

"She didn't even come close to kicking our asses," I say sourly. "Bitch is all cheap shots and weak magic. Only reason she got the upper hand is because I was caught off guard. It's easy to throw the first punch when your opponent isn't looking."

"It was hardly a fair fight," Dragan agrees.

"In fact, I'd love to see her try that shit a second time. I'd fuck her up so good we'd need a séance to hear from her again."

He grabs my hand and lays a gentle kiss on the back of it. His thumb brushes over my knuckles. "She's no match for you, my love. None of them are."

His words instantly cool my temper like a soothing balm.

Our waiter Daniel shows up with another round of drinks.

"Atta boy. Keep 'em coming," Dragan says as he leans forward to grab our cocktails, then he slips our waiter a generous tip.

Daniel nods a *thank you* and makes himself scarce. I close my eyes and listen to the sound of the waves crashing and the seagulls calling while the rays bronze my skin to a perfect, sun-kissed glow. Sometimes, Mother Nature is the best form of magic.

"Remind me to thank the Order when this is all over," I say, opening my eyes and looking over at Dragan. "If it weren't for their staggering incompetence, none of this would've happened."

He grins. "I'll be sure to remind you to say that to their faces the next time we see them."

"It would be my pleasure."

I glance down at my tits, admiring them through my shades. "Speaking of pleasure, what do you say…fancy another shag?" I ask, running my fingers along my nipples.

"Only if you promise to make it hurt."

I raise my glass. "Here's to being punished in paradise."

Dragan lifts his glass—c*link*—then he takes a slow sip and holds my gaze, his eyes burning with desire.

Yeah, we're not leaving here anytime soon.

21

REYHA

I'm trying to remember.

My mind is completely blank, but I'm trying so hard to get back to myself. I know I'm someone who is stuck here. I know I belong somewhere else, but it's all been wiped from my thoughts and memories. I don't remember a single thing. Not my middle name, not my shoe size, nothing. And it pisses me off.

Someone did this to me, and I have to get them back. I have to figure this out and save myself from whomever that dark shadow of a person is. I have no memory of him or her, just that they put the lights out and sent me into this dim and dangerous place to cause me pain.

Whoever I am, I have a temper. I can feel the rage boiling over as I walk along the crowded path, covered in sludge and grime. The rot of this place has covered me, made me one of its own, but I won't be had so easily.

I clap my hands together, hard, inflicting pain, trying to break through this fog and get back to where I was heading. I don't live in this mire. I live someplace nice, I think. I would never pick this dump, never come here willingly, so someone has dropped me off and left me to suffer.

Every inch of my body aches with cuts and sores, my blood draining slowly and mixing with the black tar-like substance that slides down the walls and covers the ground.

I continue to bang my hands together, bringing whatever sensations to the forefront that I can manage. I need a jolt to bring it back. I need pain or a terrible scare to give me back what's mine.

It's so hot, like hell's leftovers. I drag along the piles of bones and rotting carcasses, trying to hold my breath but knowing it's pointless. The smell will still be there. It's not going to go away or lessen.

The vines hanging from the sky whip at my face, tearing at my cheeks, making them sting as I keep pushing forward. No matter what, I have to keep moving in this direction. I feel like the truth is just over that seething pile of filth ahead of me, or way over there in the boiling pit of rot, or maybe beyond that.

Another vine hits me square in the mouth and I slap it away with one hand, covering my bloody mouth with the other dirty hand and I suddenly get it.

I cut myself the last time I was lucid. I left a mark of magic.

Magic?

But of course!

I rub the inside of my little finger, making a cleanish spot and I see a swirling mark, hidden from every other thing on earth, something just for me to view.

It's my reminder. I put this here so that when that pig Elias covered me in whatever spell he's got me under I'd remember at some point. And so I have.

I have power, it's just been suppressed. I've been kidnapped and that asshat has decided to make me his meek little love, but my magic knows this is nothing I'd ever want, and so it's been fighting to wake me up.

I raise my hands to the red, bleeding sky and shout out a few words that I think will help remove the darkness from my mind. I shout again and once more, taking over control of this world of death and devastation. I'm going to get out of here one way or another.

The sky cracks in an uneven split, revealing a line of gray and white that tells me that it must be evening in whatever nightmare Elias has dropped me in. I wring my hands together and shout out my commands as the black swirling pits of decay give way to green grass and trickling water.

I walk to the split in the reality and stick my hands through the crack, pulling it open, ripping pieces of his pitiful spell apart in my hands, dragging the sides down and stomping them with my filthy bare feet, the dark matter fading from my body as my magic recognizes me and pulls me out into the light, stripping the matted clothes from my body and making me clean as a preacher's sheets.

My hair is cleaned in a magical instant and left flowing in the breeze that lifts me higher, dressing me in a pale pink dress and putting slippers on my feet. My wounds are gone and the only thing left that even hints at my captivity is the new pink skin covering where my gashes and cuts used to be.

When my magic is finished righting all the wrongs of my appearance, it begins to work on my mind, bringing back the spells and memories that were stolen. It reminds me, as I'm sure it's been trying to do for some time now, of things I know, telling me the things that are now secrets between me and the power. Things I will be shown that will put me on the path to getting my witch's intellect back.

I land lightly on a bed of fragrant flowers of all colors and am made to rest while my magic watches over me, granting me peace in what has been an otherwise terrifying few weeks—at least a few weeks. How long have I been here? Where's Trixie? Where's Jameson? What else have I lost?

The questions keep coming as my eyes get heavier, and though I want to stay awake and fight on, my subconscious and my powers take over and make me rest up for the fight I'm about to pick.

22

E L I A S

I'm busy drumming up Reyha's new form of torture in a little cabin I fashioned for myself on the property. There's no way I was going to live in the filth next door; that shit's beneath me. Besides, I'm having fun orchestrating this whole thing from afar. I've been warping Reyha's sense of time, drawing out her punishment for as long as I can.

As I prepare to bring the next nightmare to life, I hear another's energy calling out to me. Frederick. He's early. This pleases me.

I ghost outside and use my powers to loosen the wards and grant him access to enter the grounds. He appears in a gust of wind. There's an ancient-looking brass box tucked beneath one arm and a spellbook resting under his other arm.

"What is this mess?" he says, repulsed as he gazes down at the toxic sludge covering his shoes.

"Here, I'll take that," I say, gesturing to the box.

As soon as my hands get close, the box repels me with a jolt.

"Not so fast," Frederick says. "You didn't think I'd come here without some assurances, did you? After that little stunt you pulled on my wife?"

"How is Alice?" I ask with fake politeness. "Feeling a little on edge lately?"

He ignores me. "I've spelled this box with a magical seal. You nor anyone else can open it without my assistance. I've also disguised the power stripping spell. You could read every page front to back in this book, but you won't find it. Not without my help."

I close my eyes and rub my fingers against my temple. "Why do you insist on making things difficult? My instructions were clear."

"I'm not taking any chances. How do I know you won't try to kill me once you get what you want?" he challenges. "We're doing things my way this time."

"And what makes you think you get to call the shots?" I ask, genuinely curious.

"First off, you're a wanted man. Everyone and their ancestors are looking for you. Secondly, you don't have the slightest idea how to work this ritual, and even if you did, you don't have the power or the skill to pull it off by yourself, which means you're in no position to be making demands."

"I should just kill you right now and save myself the future headache."

"But you won't," he says confidently. "And if you so much as whisper one hexed word my way, I'll alert the Midnight Order to your whereabouts and spoil this entire plan of yours. So if you want to slip out quietly and go unnoticed, then it'd be wise of you to keep your mouth shut and do as I say."

I don't know what it is lately. Maybe it's the condescending tone everyone likes to take with me, or the casual threats and insults they sling my way, or perhaps it's everyone's desire to make me their bitch, but I'm sick and tired of people testing my patience and abusing my good nature. That shit ends now.

I command the vines to twist up his legs, torso, arms, and neck, anchoring him in place. Before Frederick can get a word out, a thick vine slides into his mouth and down the back of his throat. He gags and chokes and struggles for air. I must have a thing for asphyxiation.

A vine squeezes his forearm, forcing him to ease his grip on the antique. I summon the box and it floats toward me and hovers in midair. I produce a dagger and walk over to him, closing in like he's prey. Reaching down, I yank the spellbook out of his other hand.

"I hate to break it to you, but you are not the only one who has the knowledge and power to perform this ritual, and I am more than willing to go out and find your replacement. Undo the seal right now," I say, pressing the tip of the blade against his skin, "or I will slit your throat and watch you bleed out like cattle, and then I will pay another visit to Alice."

Hatred fills his eyes as he struggles against the vines. Once he realizes he has no chance at fighting his way out, he lets out a garbled plea and squeezes his fist. When he reopens it, a tiny wave of blue energy releases from his palm. It hits the box and the seal crumbles.

I slip the spellbook under my arm, then grab the box and open the lid. Resting inside is an amulet of some kind. No idea what its purpose is, but I'll find out soon enough.

I pick up the object and slide it into my pocket, then I toss the antique over my shoulder and into the pool of sludge.

"There, now the scales are a little more balanced," I say, satisfied.

I release Frederick. He bends over and coughs up black goo, then he glances up at me. His look is murderous, but he's wise enough to keep his mouth shut.

"Follow me. And don't bother trying to attack me while my back is turned," I say, holding my blade up as a warning.

I use my powers to create a pathway from here to the front door. I say a spell to undo the mystical locks, and the front door gently swings open on its own, inviting me inside to be reunited with the love of my life.

This is it. Our moment. Our time. Our forever.

A mixture of hope and excitement stirs inside me. I feel like I'm walking down the aisle, ready to give Reyha my vows and lay down my life at her feet. This is my do-over. My second chance at happiness.

From now on, I'm looking at everything through fresh eyes, pure and reborn.

With each step I take, the darkness around me fades. The pool of black tar swirls away, and vibrant flowers and long, green grasses emerge. The vines and tendrils slither down the house and recede into the ground. As my foot hits the front step, the wood magically refurbishes itself. The walls inside return to a pristine white, and every piece of furniture is restored. The animal carcasses rapidly decompose until there is nothing left behind, and the smell of rot and decay is replaced with subtle traces of jasmine and rose.

Speaking of flowers…

I conjure up the most beautiful bouquet of white roses to present to her. I step inside the cottage and search the kitchen, the living room, the bathroom, but no Reyha.

"She must be upstairs. I'll go grab her and bring her down. You wait here," I tell Frederick.

"It's best to perform the ceremony outside," he replies. "The more power I can pull from nature, the better chance she has at surviving the extraction."

I nod and head upstairs. Reyha will survive the ritual. Of this, I have no doubt. I check every room, every corner of the house. She's nowhere to be found. *How can this be?* A wave of panic hits me. I drop the bouquet, grip the spellbook, and race down the stairs, plowing past Frederick and barreling through the back door.

"Reyha!" I yell repeatedly, frantically searching for any sign of her in the yard.

She's gone. How did she escape? And how the fuck did I not sense it? Before I can even think, Frederick ghosts in front of me and blasts me with a wave of energy. I'm instantly knocked to the ground, the spellbook tumbling out of my hands. Blood trickles from my nose and drips onto the grass.

I make a move to stand, but Frederick hits me with another wave of energy. And then another. And then one more. I crawl along the ground in a pathetic attempt to escape his onslaught. He marches over and grabs my shirt collar, yanking me upright. Giving me a taste of my own medicine, he grips my throat with such force that soon I begin to struggle for air. This is how much he despises me. Instead of using magic to finish the job, he's opted to use his bare hands. I'm impressed. To him, this is personal.

I grab his wrist and try to wrestle him off, but his hold is too strong. Instinctively, I reach down and produce another dagger. I struggle and fight and flail, letting Frederick think he's got me. His lips curl into a smug smile, playing right into my hands.

Right before I lose consciousness, I thrust the blade into his gut. He lets out a loud cry and freezes, releasing his hold on my neck. I suck in a breath and rip the dagger back out and slit his throat, a spray of blood painting the grass.

He drops to his knees and struggles in silence. Our faces are mere inches apart, and I watch as the panic in his eyes slowly fades to vacancy. He slips his hand in his pocket, and then his limp body falls to the ground.

I sit back on my knees, panting and struggling to catch my breath. Once I can think clearly, I stand on shaky legs. I send Frederick's body flying straight through the back door and into the house. I conjure a giant ball of fire and hurl it at the cottage, setting the whole thing ablaze. If I can't have what I want, then I'll burn it all to the fucking ground. As for Alice, her curse will remain intact—my final "fuck you" to Frederick.

I bend over to pick up the spellbook, wiping Frederick's blood off the cover. I glance up and watch as the flames lick the sky. Mesmerized yet furious beyond words, the rage inside me builds with every crackle and pop the fire produces.

Then, I disappear and begin the hunt for Reyha.

23

TRIXIE

Reyha's loose!

The stunning declaration hits me in the side of my head, alerting me to the fact that something has shifted and she's either not hidden any longer or she's made a hole in the spell that's kept her. I can feel her. Her magic is probably wondering what's taken me so long and is likely pissed off.

I reach into one of my jacket pockets and grab a handful of tracking powder. It's the dullest shade of green I've ever seen, but it should do the trick. I fight to get it out in time and toss it clumsily into the air, needing it to latch onto Reyha's bit of freedom and lead me to her before all I can do is be pissed at myself for not reacting fast enough.

But her essence lingers. It's not hurried as if she's struggling to get away or running for her life; it's light and airy. It's not what I expected at all, and I'm trying to figure out what the fuck is happening because this doesn't make sense. This is a witchcraft Code Red…at least it should be.

The wave lifts up on a breeze, the only connection I have to Reyha about to fade right out of sight. I wave my arms maniacally, blowing and shooing the tracking powder up into the air, knowing if I don't work quickly that it will fall flat and I'll lose the trail.

I don't know if Elias knows she's free, or if not *free*, at least able to communicate in whatever fashion she can, so I have to work fast. Maybe all she's been able to do is stick her hand out the window and wave it around. Whatever it is, however much she can do, it's all I need.

I follow the wind and the gray-green dust of my own design, begging it to do its thing, pleading with it to attach and show me the what and the where. I look like a fool to the folks stopping to watch me chase nothing. I look homeless, no question. Crazy, absolutely, but I'm not here for them.

I stumble as I run to keep up with the vibe that could spell the end of this nightmare. It's not that I'm afraid to lose it, it's that I *can't* lose it. To waste this opportunity would be to lose everything. I can't get on with my life until Reyha is able to get on with hers. We're tied together and knotted into each other's lives.

I have my dream man at the house, waiting for my return, waiting to meet Reyha, waiting to begin our life together. I know Jameson is waiting as well. We all wait. We all hate it, but this is my one chance, and I'm exactly the girl who can bring this to an end. It makes my mouth water to think about getting Reyha away from Elias and having his plans spoiled. Again. What a fucking loser. He's truly someone who has let love make a fool of him.

Unrequited love, that is.

I continue to run after the wisp of Reyha's magic that waves at me, showing me it's here and what I need to recognize. I reach in for the last bit of powder I have and toss it, knowing it's now or never, not that I'd give up. No, no. I'll never give up.

With all strength and height I have I leap into the air with the spell in my hand, calling out to the wisp to wait up for Christ's sake, whispering words that will make it see that I'm who it's looking for, in case it doesn't already know. I am rewarded with the last warm bit of the tendril wrapping around my wrist and pulling me up into the air with it, almost laughing at me.

Definitely laughing at me. That fucking figures. How like Reyha, and her power, to make me look dumb. Here I am, running and staggering down the sidewalk, trying to chase this last little piece of her magic, and it's having a great time at my expense. I was never going to lose it. It was playing with me.

I feel lighter than I have in some time now, knowing that her magic has her stupid sense of humor, knowing that as soon as her power was able to find me, it came right for me, and made me think it was all by chance.

I mix my own magic with hers and it lifts me up higher, settling me into the comfort only a cloud can provide as it takes me to wherever on this planet that asshole Elias has stashed Reyha.

She's gonna owe me for this. I ran. I never run. I hate running, and her magic had a good laugh at my expense not doubt.

After I kick Elias's ass, I'm gonna kick Reyha's.

24

V A L A

It's been days and there's still no sign of Reyha or Elias. We've descended the slopes, trading in the stark white for the lusher, green side of Switzerland. I wish someone would've told me that we'd be dealing with stalker cattle up here. They've been following us for ten minutes, mooing and bellowing like they're trying to shoo us off.

"Why do you draw attention everywhere we go?" Jameson says. "You're supposed to be invisible, but even the animals know you're here."

"Why do you assume it's me riling them up?" I challenge. "Maybe it's you." It's definitely me who's putting them on edge, but still. It's the principle of it.

Jameson stops up ahead and reaches into the duffel. I hang back and scope out our surroundings while he produces his water canister and takes a swig.

"Come on, Reyha. Where are you?" I whisper, looking for anything out of the ordinary. I plead with the universe to give me a sign. Anything.

"Hey!" Jameson calls out. "Come check this out. I think I found something."

I float over to where he's standing. Not far off in the distance, I see the remnants of a building or a house, one that's been burned to the ground.

Jameson and I exchange a knowing look and head in that direction. As we get closer to the rubble, an invisible force repels me. My ghostly essence flickers like a light going in and out, and all my instincts and magical signals get scrambled.

"Son of a bitch," I say, shaking off the annoying effects.

Elias.

"Are you all right?" Jameson asks.

"I'm fine," I say, irritated. "Stand back."

He takes a few steps back, giving me clearance.

I raise my hands and chant, working to bring down the barrier. I recite the spell over and over, praying that it takes. Finally, on the fifth try, the forcefield comes tumbling down.

I cautiously float onto the property until I reach the pile of rubble and ash. The few identifiable pieces of house that are left are charred and covered in soot.

Jameson bends down and holds his hand out over the debris. "It's still warm," he says, staring up at me. He swallows hard. "You don't think Reyha...?" He can't even bear to finish the thought.

"No, I don't think she's dead," I say, though I'm more confused than ever. If Reyha got out, I should be able to sense her magic. So why can't I?

Maybe we're still too far behind her. Or maybe she cloaked herself to ensure Elias wouldn't find her. Did she escape and burn the house down while Elias was stuck inside? Or was it Elias who torched this place?

Or did someone else get here first?

As I try my best to piece together what the hell happened, Jameson sets the duffel on the ground and steps onto the rubble. He lifts a plank and tosses it to the side. Then he grabs a large section of wall and flips it over.

"What are you doing?" I ask.

"Searching for any bodies. I want to make sure we uncover all the evidence before we leave here."

I wave my hands and start flinging posts, heavy stones, and charred figurines into the air, scattering them across the yard, eager to speed this process up.

We spend the next several minutes sifting through the debris. Who knows what potions or herbs or spellbooks we could've had access to had we found this place in a better state, before those items were ruined or disintegrated. As we're making headway, I use my powers to lift a giant pile of stones, and right beneath it lies someone's remains.

Jameson's fist flies to his mouth.

"Don't puke on the body," I warn in mock seriousness. "That's in poor taste."

He immediately looks away, fighting to keep his lunch down.

What's left of this person screams male, and a tinge of hope flares inside me at the thought that it might be Elias.

"You stay here and keep digging. I'm going to search the yard for any signs or clues—something that will help lead us to Reyha. If you find anyone else buried under all this shit, holler."

Before he can respond, I vanish and reappear near the property line. I float along at a snail's pace, keeping a close eye out.

When I reach the backyard, I notice a shallow puddle of red. I glide over to it and hold out my hand. Scarlet whisps begin to rise up and delicately swirl around my palm. I let my magic study the blood, inspecting it for any trace of familiarity, trying to make out if I can recognize who this person was. Nothing noteworthy pops up, which is a relief and a disappointment.

Relief because it's not Reyha's blood.

Disappointment because it's not Elias's.

No, this essence belongs to someone I've never met. Probably the dude resting underneath all the debris. He was magical, that much my senses can gather, but that's as far as the blood takes me.

Once Jameson and I have examined every last scrap of building and blade of grass, he grabs our stuff and we take off, hopefully not too far behind Reyha.

25

TRIXIE

She's gonna owe me her first born child for this.

How far away did he take her? Out of the time zone for sure, but off-world maybe. I've been traveling for hours, floating through the atmosphere in the rain and the sunlight as my powers fight with hers for control of the narrative.

I'm soaked and starving but I'll make it. Her magic is more mischievous than mine, and I know that's why this is such a hard journey. Her magic is angry with me, at least I think so. It's the vibe I'm picking up as it surrounds me, making me feel like we're about to square up in an alley for turf rights.

My magic is strong though and is protecting me from what her magic would like to do to me for being late to come after her. I can't explain myself to the magical attitude that is giving me the side-eye, but when we get to Reyha she will undoubtedly understand that I have been doing my damnedest to save her silly ass.

She'll know that I would never leave her, that I will always come for her.

Or will she?

The last time we spoke, we fought.

Obviously Elias was watching us closely, but I didn't realize how closely. He was next door, up a tree, on the wind, doing all he could to find his chance to take us out, but first, he'd want to have his fun, and so he did.

With me.

I'm going to say he's had Reyha too, whether by force or by trickery I can't say yet, maybe both, maybe neither.

The gloves are off, that's for sure, and the first opportunity I get, I'll kill him. Call it murder if you like, but it's self-defense and no one can convince me differently.

I'm so fucking done with live and let live. He doesn't let us live, he lets us run and hide, and live in the fear that he'll find us and kill us. I no longer care about Reyha's wishes to just avoid him. He won't leave well enough alone, and so I have no choice.

I can picture it, his life leaving his body. The light leaving his eyes as he becomes just another dead guy ready to rot away into the background, no longer here, no longer able to hurt us, or anyone else. His fine cigars left unsmoked, his expensive bourbon dumped down the drain as I feel the giddy excitement of destroying things he takes pleasure in. I will erase all evidence he ever existed. He'll be nothing more than a bare bit of memory that will invade my consciousness briefly now and again, as if dust has been stirred up and blown about, and I'll wipe it away with the smallest swipe of the back of my hand as I get back to the book I would be reading, or the spell I would be perfecting.

Eventually, he will never enter my mind again. Or Reyha's. She'll thank me one day for killing him. Unless she's already done it herself, which seems unlikely, but not impossible.

I hope he's not dead yet. That would be anticlimactic at this point. Simply walking up to the bad guy and putting a bullet in his head is too good for him. It's why the heroes in movies always have to come back and win the big fight at the end. We need that sense of justice, that feeling of satisfaction that the asshole in the story, the one who's caused all the damage and drama, gets an ending that we can live with.

I want that feeling of justice. I need to have it, and so I pray with all my heart and soul that Reyha and I get to end him together, that she's come over to my side and is done with trying to be tolerant of this monster and burn him alive.

The idea of containing him in a witch ball isn't appetizing at all. I don't want him locked away to serve his sentence for his crime against humanity or the witching community. He could possibly find a way back from that if the right dark warlock found him and helped him to reanimate.

No, not for our dear Elias. It's going to be as if he never existed. He's going to be erased and there won't be a single hair off his pointed little head left on this earth.

My mind begins to race with a new spell that we might be able to use, after we beat him to death first. A spell that will erode his fingerprints off anything he's ever touched, his dandruff, everything that he might have shed in the course of his evil life. All of it—gone.

It isn't necessary to have all that gone so he can't return; it's only for my own sense of outrage that I will take his legacy, his everything away from this world and leave others wondering how I did it and if I would ever use it on them.

Perhaps that will make those bitches of the Midnight Order think twice about sending another assassin after us.

Probably not, but it's worth a shot.

26

R E Y H A

My muscles are protesting by the time I make it far enough into the woods. It's pitch-black outside and hiding in the forest seemed like the safest option while I recover. I'm less vulnerable here and less easy to find. At least that's what I'm hoping.

My magic healed all my physical wounds, but now I'm drawing on nature to replenish my powers. I nearly jump out of my skin every time the leaves rustle or an animal scurries, half-expecting to turn around and see Elias standing behind me. I have no idea how much time has passed since he kidnapped me, but it feels like it's been ages.

I'm sure he's figured out by now that I'm missing and he's on his way to collect me and drag me back to that house of horrors as we speak. Not gonna happen.

Addressing all the recent trauma I've endured will have to wait. I'm choosing to block it out as best I can. There's no time to confront any of it. I need to kill Elias and eliminate the threat first, then I'll have all the time in the world to put myself back together again.

There's going to be hell to pay when I see him.

I press my hand against my stomach and conjure a tiny, subtle glow in my palm, being mindful not to let it shine too bright. I bend down and search along the forest floor for herbs, flowers, or any other random ingredients that I could use in a pinch.

The one upside to this ridiculous outfit I'm wearing is it's easy to move around in. I know magic has a mind of its own, but seriously, what was mine thinking when it threw together a pale pink dress and fuzzy slippers as my escape outfit? As soon as I get enough strength back, I'm poofing out of this silly little costume and into something more appropriate.

Suddenly, I'm interrupted by a familiar force. I stow away my light, knowing what's closing in overhead before I even have time to look up and witness it.

A mystical cloud rolls in, preparing to shower me with a storm named Trixie. As it approaches, my magic evaporates a little too early and dumps her right over a large pine tree.

"Ah! Fuck!" she hollers.

Branches tear and snap as she falls, the sound echoing through the forest and startling the wildlife. A slew of profanities escapes her lips. I can't see much of anything, but I hear her getting whacked and smacked and clubbed all the way down.

Her body hits the ground. She groans and sits up slowly, pine needles sticking out of her deep red hair. She looks like a damn porcupine.

The woman really knows how to make an entrance.

"Well, look who finally decided to show up," I say, walking up to her and placing my hands on my hips. "What took you so long?"

27

T R I X I E

"What took me so long? Are you fucking kidding me with that?"

"Not really. I thought you'd be here days ago," she says, and I wonder which way this conversation is going to go.

"You know, I'm not going to do this with you. I came here to finish Elias and end the nightmares associated with his pitiful existence. Are you in, or are you too busy playing pretty princess in that ridiculous getup?"

"I'm working on it. I'm not that strong just yet. I've had my memory all but erased, but it's coming back. I see some of my power left to seek you out, so once that reattaches I should be stronger still. A little bit at a time," she says.

And now I feel like an asshole. "Here," I say, handing over the bag off my back, letting her see that I packed for her.

She digs around inside and her face lights up. She looks at me and I know this is that moment I've dreaded. And looked forward to.

She lunges forward and hugs me and all the hostility that friends can have toward each other when we're pissed off melts away and we get through the awkwardness, hugging and crying and professing how much we love each other and how scared we've been that the other was harmed, or the other thing that I can't bring myself to say. No longer of this world. Gone for all time. The "D" word. I won't say it. I won't even think it. It's too scary.

How long we stand there and hug and cry is anyone's guess, but I keep my ears open for the sound of Elias's approach. I hear and sense nothing, so we hug on.

"I thought you were dead," she says as she kisses my cheek and pushes back, pulling clothes from the bag and holding them to her face, breathing in the smell of our home and finding some peace in that.

"Me?"

"Yeah, you. Do you not remember how we left things?"

"I do, but I don't think we need to go into it," I say, really not wanting to discuss how wrong I was.

"Hmmmph," is all she says, knowing that I remember just fine, understanding that I'm gonna take responsibility for every bit of my bad behavior, and acknowledging that this is as much of an apology as I can muster.

She strips out of the fluffy ballerina rags and into some underthings. Next it's tight jeans and tennis shoes, an old T-shirt from a music festival we went to fifty years ago, and the oldest and most comfortable sweatshirt she owns. She looks like her old self and I feel calmness return.

"You packed for the weather. How'd you know it was cold where I was?" she asks.

"I didn't. There are shorts and sandals at the bottom of the bag. I knew Elias had you, and I didn't see his arrogant ass taking you anywhere but Europe because it's *so sophisticated*. He's predictable."

"Sort of. I never saw him tricking me into fucking him. That's a new one," she says and shivers at the disgusting memory.

"Same, girl. Same."

Her eyes grow huge. "No!" she says, anger evident in her every movement.

"Yup. I thought I was in love with a great guy, and we had the most amazing, meaningful, dirty sex I've ever had, and it wasn't Finn. It was Elias disguised as Finn. I want to shower and peel my skin off. Good news is I know exactly what to do about this," I say with a nod.

"Yeah? You know how we can fuck him up good? Make him feel all the disgust we feel?"

"You bet I do. He thinks I'm dead. As far as he's concerned, he murdered me in the fight we had at his place. I brought the fucking house down on both of us. I broke every doorway and piece of furniture. I almost had him, too, and he knows it. I know what we can do, you bet, and then we kill him. And I won't have any discussion on that again. He's pushed me just as far as I'm going to go," I say, and I see that she agrees with me this time.

He dies at the end.

28

ELIAS

I've been tracking Reyha to no avail. Just when I get a faint whiff of her essence, it dissipates, leaving the trail cold. I have no idea what kind of condition she's in, but I'm betting my magic is still blocking her memory. She's probably wandering around somewhere nearby, lost and confused. I have to find her. Until then, I must keep my head together.

I stop running and wrestle the spellbook into my hands. I quickly flip through the pages until something—anything—jumps out at me. Maybe there's a spell in here that can help me find her.

"*Sublucetote*," I command.

The words light up on the page, helping me see. Now that Reyha has escaped, there's no time to find somebody else to perform the ritual. It must be me.

It's always been me.

As I'm flipping away, a drawing catches my eye on one of the pages. Right beneath the incantation, there's a picture of an amulet. It looks exactly like the one I stole from Frederick. I reach into my back pocket, slide the artifact out, and hold it up next to the page. The image is identical. I search all the other pages to see if it shows up anywhere else in this book. It doesn't. This leads me to believe I've found what I'm looking for.

Frederick was an idiot *and* a liar. He never disguised the power-stripping spell—it's right here in front of me. Can nobody tell the truth anymore? Why would he lie? As if I wouldn't have found out eventually. Perhaps when I killed him, it broke the spell he cast to hide it from me. What a joke. I should've killed him sooner.

I slip the amulet back inside my pocket and study the incantation carefully. It's short in length, so that's a plus. Easy to memorize. When I find Reyha, it'll be right on the tip of my tongue.

I spend the next few minutes reading how this ritual is supposed to work. It puts me on edge knowing I'm winging this part, but what other choice do I have? Frederick is dead, Reyha is loose, the Midnight Order is out to kill me, and Karina and Dragan have ghosted me, leaving me to fix this mess all on my own. And fix it, I will.

The instructions are clear: Once the ritual begins, the object is placed on the recipient's chest and used to extract the powers. The spellcaster recites the incantation until all the magic has been stripped from the recipient. Afterward, the magic is either stored within the amulet, or it can be absorbed by another magical practitioner.

Interesting. Now I understand why this secret is so well-guarded. This spell doesn't erase magic, it transfers it. Meaning, I could steal Reyha's power and combine it with my own. My heart races at the thought. And unlike the witch balls, this amulet doesn't discriminate. It will absorb any magic—dark, light, or other.

No wonder Frederick and the others wanted to keep this information hidden. I'll bet they've been using this knowledge to their advantage the entire time, boosting themselves with power and keeping everyone else beneath them and in the dark, all the while spouting cautionary tales of performing this type of ritual. Who knows how much power they've stolen over the years. The blatant hypocrisy sickens me. Does the Midnight Order know about this? Hell, they're probably in on it.

Towards the bottom of the page, there's a warning about the toll this takes on the caster. If they aren't powerful enough to complete the ritual, they risk draining their magic in the process and dying. No surprise there. The bigger the spell, the heavier the toll.

Frederick was right about one thing: a full moon would've been ideal. But something tells me I'm powerful enough to pull this off on my own, and I'm betting Frederick knew that. Still, I'll need to replenish my strength afterward.

I slam the book shut and close my eyes for a moment, trying to clear my head and put myself in Reyha's shoes. If I were wandering around, scared and alone and confused, where would I go? I come up with two likely scenarios: either she showed up at a stranger's house to ask for help, or she headed into the forest. It's the middle of the night and there are hardly any houses around. And if she's wounded, her magic would naturally lead her to the forest for healing and protection. My gut tells me to ghost there and keep searching.

I say a spell to shrink the spellbook to travel size and slip it into my front pocket.

Then off I go.

29

LENA

I know what I have to do, but damn it, I wasn't supposed to have to be involved.

Reyha's life has been forfeit for a hundred years. I know it. She knows it. We all know it. But the fact that she's my niece makes it even harder.

The daughter of my sister should have known better than to do what she did. I blame her mercenary hetero soulmate for leading her down this path, but it makes no difference now. Action must be taken, for several reasons.

I need to claim the power she holds ransom. Her witch ball collection is legendary, and I should be proud of her. She's done things no one else could do and that was admirable, but the fact is that things have changed, and I now need to refresh my power or lose control of the coven I lead.

I *know* it's hypocritical, believe me, I know. I can't help that. Elias was supposed to kill her so that my hands remained free of her blood, but the idiot has always been in love with her so I made a bad choice there. I thought her rejection of him would fuel his desire to kill her, but it seems to have only made him want her more.

If she were dead, I'd know it. I'd feel it on the wind and in my heart. I would know. He's failed, and now I have to get my hands dirty.

We have to get our hands dirty. The Circle will have to fight with me to end Reyha and in turn, accept the power that will be released as she takes her last breath.

I need that power more than I need my sister's daughter.

I had to pick, and I made my choice. Reyha can't be controlled and therefore must be removed. My hands are tied. If she weren't so obstinate I wouldn't have to resort to such drastic measures, but she's gotten more powerful over the years and there's nothing else I can do.

I promised her mother I'd care for her and I have, to the best of my ability, but she's always been a wild child. Unthinking. Unrealistic. Pig-headed. If my teachings had taken root she'd be on my side, my second in command, but she went her own way after that unfortunate thing with Elias and Vala.

How she could take Vala's death so personally is beyond me. They used to screw around, then she was dead. So what? There's more to life than pining for your dead girlfriend.

I sit with my thoughts as I try to call my magic to the forefront but there's not much happening here. I doubt I could cause little more than a dust devil in my current condition.

If I could change time I'd be all right. I know Reyha has a spell to erase an event from existence, and I know it demands high payment, but I need that spell. I'll get it from her before the end. As long as I'm cutting her up into little pieces to get the witch balls, I'll pull this spell from her too. She won't be needing it where she's going.

If I could go back, call up the past and really make my presence known, I would be able to undo the idiocy that cost me most of my power and all of my strength. I could also stop myself from giving her the idea to hunt warlocks. I could take back those foolish words. I'd never, ever have told her about the witch balls. Never would've told her that they hold power and essence of any evil witch or warlock that gets too close. She decided to go all noble and fight that good fight and all that shit with her lifelong partner in crime. Beatrix.

My council will be here soon and I have no plan but for us to do the dirty work ourselves. I don't look for my other four witches to have come up with a plan to get what we want without having to jump in and risk pissing off the rest of our coven. I know many witches, warlocks too, that if I'm being honest, will side with Reyha, but that will never do. I'll have the power to get rid of them once she's dead and her witch balls release all that wonderful dark magic. I'll claim it all for myself, if it's at all possible. If I have to share with my council, I'll do that, but only so much of it.

I have to be the most powerful again or I risk losing my position, and being on the losing side isn't for me. I won't be someone's servant. I won't be less than I am today.

Elias has been useless, and I hope and pray that I don't have to finish him off as well. He has enough enemies that there would be a line around the block of warlocks drooling for the chance to battle him. I make a mental note to put it out there to the warlock council that he'll be up for grabs soon if anyone is interested. The fact that I know where he's at right now need not be advertised.

It's always been me.

I've always been the one behind her tragedies, her failures, her broken heart. I'm able to hide my disdain behind being Aunty Lena, but enough's enough. Though I love Reyha, my survival depends on her demise.

And I have a lot of will to live.

30

E L I A S

The forest is teeming with life tonight. I'm quick yet stealthy as I work through the maze of trees, wanting to avoid scaring Reyha off.

I weave through several rows of trunks until I come across a large open space in the middle of the forest, trees towering over me in every direction. Once I stop moving, I hear a scattering of noises coming from the underbrush. I follow the sounds, being careful not to give my position away. I inch closer to finding the source.

The noises stop.

And so do I.

A twig snaps behind me and I spin around, half-expecting to see something or someone, but nothing's there.

Then I catch a glimpse of a short figure with long, blonde hair.

Reyha.

As I make my way toward her, something else breezes past me, producing a fierce gust of wind and knocking me off balance. I straighten my spine and glance over to Reyha, only to see that she's gone.

What the hell?

"Reyha?" I call out.

My eyes dart this way and that, ready for whatever's lurking out here in the shadows waiting to terrorize Reyha and me. I must protect her at all costs. She's still under my influence, which means she's defenseless against our visitor.

Suddenly, the figure materializes. I launch a ball of magic in its direction, but I miss and hit a tree as my opponent vanishes. Dark lines appear on the bark and crawl upward, spreading over the trunk like cracks in glass. The tree groans and creaks and snaps as if it's bursting from the inside. It begins to fall, and I ghost out of its path and reappear on the opposite side. It collides with another hulking spruce and finally crashes to the forest floor with a loud *thud.*

"Enough!" I shout. "Come out and face me."

The forest goes eerily quiet for several beats. All I can hear is my heart pounding in my ears, my senses on high alert, ready to defend and strike and kill.

I hear the slightest noise off to the side, but I'm distracted when I see Reyha again. She's standing several feet away, her back turned to me.

"Reyha!"

She glances over her shoulder and starts running when she sees me.

Shit, she doesn't recognize who I am.

Before she can disappear from my sight, I race to catch up with her.

"Wait, darling, stop! It's me!"

She picks up the pace, gliding through trees with ease. I bust my ass, running faster and faster until I'm right on her heels. Up ahead, there's a giant log blocking the path. She swerves out of the way and stumbles, but I keep heading straight for it. I hear her panting harder, more desperate for breath, and I know it's out of fear and not fatigue.

I use the log to propel myself into the air and make a dive for Reyha, tackling her to the ground. She twists and flips beneath my weight, trying to wrestle her way out of my hold.

"Damn it, quit fighting me. I'm not going to hurt you," I tell her.

She continues to struggle.

I roll her onto her back until she's staring up at me. I immediately freeze, too stunned to form words.

Beatrix?

A sickening wave of confusion washes over me, and she begins to laugh. She snaps her fingers and her hair changes from blonde to red, starting at the root and flowing all the way down to the tip.

"Suprise, asshole."

31

R E Y H A

To say that Trixie is a diabolical genius doesn't do her crazy ass justice. I'm glad she's on my side.

We stand at the edge of the forest and take a few cleansing breaths, sucking in the freshness and purity of the lovely nature that surrounds us, exhaling all the evil and fear that's covered us that we never even knew was here.

In with the grass and flowers, out with Elias and his wicked trickery. In with the knowledge that I'm on the right side, out with any fear I have that this will not go my way.

Even despicable, disgraced warlocks have a code of conduct, but this asshole has thrown that out the window along with every other trait people with a soul have.

Soulless. That describes him perfectly, it seems.

"Ready?" she asks, a smile across her lips, her excitement about her plan exudes from her face, her hands, and I can hear her heart beating faster.

I feel the same way. The two of us united can do anything, we can take anyone down, we can fix the wrongs and go on about our lives. We used to do this in the past, but only as vigilantes. We only ever went after the witches and warlocks who were utterly irredeemable, the most foul of the bunch. The ones the law couldn't, or wouldn't, take care of themselves.

I have stored all their powers in my witch balls, never to give it over, never to let it loose. I could store Elias's power too. I might have to. I surely don't want his magic. He's touched me enough, never again. Trixie won't want it, I'm certain of that.

"What do you want to do with his magic when we off him? I don't want it; I assume you don't either."

"Oh, I want it. You bet your sweet ass I want it. I want him to know that he's beat and that we did it and that I'm going to be the one to benefit from his death, more than others would. If you took his power, he might be okay with it because of that twisted *love* thing he has for you. But me? Oh dude, that'll turn him inside out," she laughs, taking another deep breath and whooshing it out.

"You know there's no going back if you accept that magic, right?"

"Yes, I know. I've been around as long as you have. I know the rules, but if we can suck that power out of him and not let it get into the hands of other evil beings, we've won," she says, clearly getting irritated with me.

"Yes, we'd win, but if we slap him into a witch ball, he's gone for good and you don't have to ever let him touch you again."

"We never *let* him touch us, but I know what you meant. To take his power, absolutely against his will, well, that's how we rape him back, so to speak," she says, a dirty little twinkle in her eye. And while I loathe the idea of this line of thinking for myself, I say Trixie has found a way to heal herself.

"Okay, that's fine, as long as you accept all the consequences. Swear it to me now. Swear that you won't change your mind and want him out of your skin."

"He isn't going to be in my skin. I'm taking only his power and turning it into mine. He will cease to exist in every way. I'll take all his treachery and deceit, and it'll never be heard from again. He'll leave no legacy; he'll have no followers to hunt for his *lost magic* or whatever the zealots would call it. We will destroy him in every way possible."

"Swear it."

"I swear I'll never ask you to help me rid myself of the trophy magic I plan to usurp," she says.

I shake my head, but if anyone can make good on this promise, it's Trixie. She's going to let him die knowing she's gotten the better of him, way worse than he got her. His violation of her will fade, from both of us, but she'll have taken back her power by taking his.

It's a lot of symmetry.

"Okay, so, we have our plan. Good enough. Now, you run that way—you're the star, so make it loud and obvious. I'll go the opposite way, and once I hear you marching through the forest, I know he'll have heard it. I'll do my thing just like we discussed and as long as we both remember that all good plans fall to shit and that we'll have to think on our feet, we should be good," she says, her excitement palpable.

"I'm ready, sis. Let's get on with it," I say as I reach for her hand and squeeze it.

She squeezes back and we're ready.

I take off running. I step on every stick I see, kicking leaves and stomping as if I'm a kid jumping in puddles. I make loud breathing noises as I run, as if this is wearing me out and I'm going to collapse any minute. I'm doing my best to play frantic without overdoing it. I'm not much of an actress, but I'm going to give it my best.

I run on, not looking around, that's Trixie's job. She's the eyes, I'm the prize. He's going to be so focused on me that she will be completely overlooked. Well, not completely. She's going to run the same race I'm running but with a different objective.

I see a flash of light to the side and I run faster still, stopping to hide in the shadow of a large oak. I squeeze in close and whisper a few words that disguise me as bark and leaves.

He runs past, yelling for me. Calling me things like *darling* and *dear,* and if I weren't already grossed out, I would be now. That sniveling, whiny little bitch voice of his makes me want to jump out of my hiding place and cut his damn throat.

But I hold.

Trixie's on and she's gonna kill it.

I hear him leaving my vicinity, running to her, thinking she's me and it gives me a burst of pure joy in my chest that he's falling for it.

So far.

I hear things crashing all around. A tree hits the ground, shaking everything in this dense wood. I can feel the breeze from the fall, and it brings me a fresh whiff of strength.

It's my turn to run again, keep up the confusion, make him wonder what in the actual hell's going on.

He's too arrogant to think there could be something going on. He thinks it's just poor lil ol' Reyha, floundering in the nightmare he created for her. Lost and afraid, unable to break free without his help.

I've got news for him.

Prick.

I know by now Trixie has hidden herself as I did and he'll now see glimpses of me, the real me, rushing in between the trees and down the little hills and over the bubbling creeks. He'll come back this way, wondering how I got from there to here.

I'd love to play at this all day, but eventually he'll catch on that someone's helping me and that I've come out of my forced amnesia, ready to fight, ready to fuck him up good.

This is the last time I hide, once Trixie gets him running back this way, I take over and get back what he owes me.

Peace. Life. Freedom. All the things that have been taken by him in one way or another.

She's bringing him this way. Tripping and struggling, I hear her gasping and acting like she's afraid, and I think she's overdoing her role as me. I don't sound like that. She could at least do me justice.

And just like she planned, he catches her, and I step out.

He moves to roll *me* over, seeing the face of my friend, the one he thought he killed. Trixie.

He staggers backward with surprise on his face, and fear. I've never seen fear there; I like it.

He turns to run, or look for me, or something, when I step out from my place of concealment and hold up my hand in a defensive stance and we're face to face.

He's so startled that he can hardly form words, but then he lunges at me in a move I didn't expect, holding what can only be a magic conducting artifact.

He's looking to take my magic, as we had planned to take his, but taking his involved killing him. He wants me weak so I have to remain with him, so I will be under his control, under his obscene power.

I fight him with all that I have, shouting for Trixie to help me and to stop him from speaking his incantation. The panic in my voice brings her to her feet, but she's too late. He's cast it. He held it to my chest and spit out a few words that I barely heard, and I felt a great shift in my body, a surge that can only mean one thing.

He got me.

I scream at the loss of my power, unable to comprehend a life without my skills. Trixie understands too as she falls to her knees and lets out a scream that says all I feel.

I'm no longer me. I'm no longer anything.

Elias staggers backward, leaning against a tree, laughing at his victory.

Trixie looks from him to me, and I see her devastation. I feel it in my own heart. She'd fight him right here and now, and she might win this time, but she's too shocked and destroyed to do much more than let a single tear slide down her cheek.

He laughs louder, not able to form words either, like Trixie, like me, but for an entirely different reason. His joy is overflowing. He's disabled me and he's damaged her. We'll no longer be a team. We'll stay friends, of course, but I'll be dead weight hanging from her neck.

I'll be nothing.

I look him over—his deep satisfaction, his happiness—and I want him dead more now than I ever have in my entire life.

I pull my now ordinary, non-magical hands to my face, looking at the long scars on my palms and the small ones on my fingers when blue flames burst from my fingertips.

I'm not powerless.

I think I misunderstood what happened here.

I think he made me more powerful, though completely unintentional.

"Interesting. I've never been able to do that before. Elias, I think whoever made you that spell pulled a fast one on you. I hope you didn't pay much for it," I say as I hold my palms out toward him and let rip a bit of my new awesomeness.

I can't wait to take the new me out for a spin, but first, to business.

32

REYHA

Blue flames erupt from my palms, and I light Elias's ass up like a raging wildfire. I hit him with everything I've got, over and over again. Patches of clothing disintegrate beneath my magic, burning away as his exposed skin begins to char and sizzle, causing him to scream and writhe in pain.

The sound of it stokes my own inner fire.

I want him to suffer. When he takes his final breath, I want the triumphant look on my face to be the last thing he ever sees.

I command the tree branches to swat him like a pesky mosquito, and his body goes sailing into the dark. I run over to him, flame in hand, but before I can touch his face and burn it all to hell, he says a command and tree roots rise from the ground and trip me. I stumble forward and catch myself, and the flame in my palm extinguishes.

He steps over me and fists the back of my hair in his hand, then slams my forehead into the ground, causing blood to spill. He yanks my head back and forces me up onto my knees, my throat fully exposed. He holds out a hand as if to conjure something, but I summon my flame around my fist and throw the hardest punch I can manage, hoping to knock loose the few screws he has left. I can practically hear them rattling around inside that empty head of his.

He staggers backward and cups the side of his face. His eyes find mine, and I rise to my feet.

"Is that all you've got?" he taunts.

"Let's find out, shall we?"

I channel my anger and inner turmoil and use it to summon my most powerful magic. Before I can even comprehend how it happens, the witch inside me takes over and releases a torrent of light and blue fire at Elias. My stream of magic covers his face and body, yet even through the flames I can hear his primal screams ripping through the forest.

Elias ghosts behind me in a flash. He whispers a dark curse, and a cloud of black smoke envelops me and enters through my mouth and nostrils. I grip the sides of my head and drop to my knees in agony. The pain is so intense it feels like my head is going to explode. I can barely breathe or think.

In my periphery, I see an orange ball of energy hit him square in the face, and his hold on me breaks before he can finish what he started. I lean forward on my hands and knees, coughing up billows of black smoke, my magic expelling his curse from my body.

"My turn," Trixie interrupts, stepping between Elias and me, eager to join in on the fun. "I just want you to know that I'll be taking your power after we vanquish your sorry ass," she tells him.

He straightens and wipes the blood from his nose. "Keep dreaming, bitch."

He chants and a cyclone appears on the forest floor, kicking up all kinds of dirt and debris and flinging it around to temporarily blind Trixie. She counter chants and the twister's contents blast outward, leaves and twigs and branches flying in every direction like a bomb went off.

Elias uses his forearm to shield his face, and Trixie lunges at him and proceeds to give him hell.

Elias flips Trixie onto her back and hits her with a dense cloud of dark magic. She coughs and waves her hands in front of her face, frantically trying to shoo it all away. He steps forward and she bends both her legs and kicks him right in the gut, channeling magic through her feet, causing him to fly backward. His body slams into a large oak, snapping one of its limbs upon impact.

Trixie scrambles to her feet, eager to keep scrapping.

Elias stands on shaky legs. His face looks ashen and sunken in, his essence barely hanging on by a thread.

I step forward to finish the job, but he goes sailing into another tree.

Trixie and I glance at each other, confused.

"Was that you?" she asks.

"No. You?"

She shakes her head.

Before Elias can get to his feet, his body rockets upward and he's ripped through thick walls of branches and leaves. He continues to get flung around in the air like a rag doll, hitting every target in sight, too weak to fight back or do much of anything. Finally, the unseen force releases him in midair, and he drops to the ground.

I hear bones snap the second he lands, and he cries out in agony.

"Now!" a female voice shouts.

Footsteps rapidly approach. Trixie and I stand on guard, ready for whatever's racing through the trees and heading our way. But nothing could prepare me for what I see next.

Jameson emerges, his pockets stuffed with bricks of black tourmaline. He holds up a witch ball, and a searing light blankets the forest.

"No!" Elias shouts, positively livid, but it's too late. The sphere has taken hold of him and there's no going back. He desperately tries to fight the pull, but dark vapors begin to seep out of his eyes, ears, mouth, and nose, drifting toward Jameson.

Trixie and I give each other a nod and conjure our power. Together, we deliver one swift, final blow. His skeletal figure slams against the base of a tree, and his essence pours out of his body, Elias too weak to house it any longer. Particles and black vapors continue to get sucked through the air and float toward Jameson, settling into the glass sphere. Once every last bit of Elias's power is trapped inside, the glow fades, and all that's left is a black wave of energy swirling around inside the orb—that and Elias's corpse chilling on the forest floor.

"Damn, now how's that for some retribution!" Trixie exclaims. She runs up to Jameson and sticks her hand out, eagerly awaiting the witch ball. "Hand it over, champ."

He laughs and passes her the sphere. She twirls her new trophy in her hands, unable to contain her excitement.

"You came?" I whisper in disbelief, staring at Jameson.

He smiles broadly. "Of course. We've been searching for you since day one. Once we heard the tree fall and all the commotion, we came as fast as we could."

"We?" I ask, confused.

Just then, Vala floats forward.

I suck in a sharp breath, unable to wrap my brain around what I'm seeing.

"Nicely done, pretty boy," she says to Jameson, paying me no mind whatsoever.

"Vala?" I say softly.

She freezes and looks at me, completely taken aback. "Rey? You can see me?"

Overwhelmed with emotion, I laugh and cry all at once. I'm so moved by these three people and their love for me, I couldn't contain it if I tried.

"You're here? How?"

She glides over in a rush, stopping a few inches from my face. "I'm so sorry. This was all my fault. I tried to keep him away, but he got past me. It was my job to protect you, and I failed. I nearly died all over again when I saw him take you, Rey. I was so scared we'd never get you back."

"Me? What about you? You paid the ultimate price, and all because I couldn't make it to you in time. I've carried that guilt with me since the day you died."

"Don't. There's no use in going down this road. What happened to me was never your fault, so stop carrying that burden. All that matters is Elias is dead. Justice has been served, and balance has been restored. I'm just grateful you can see me. I've been waiting for this moment for so long. I've rehearsed this conversation thousands of times, trying to figure out what I'd say to you if you ever got the chance to see me again. But now that the moment is here, all I want to do is hug you and I can't."

"I know the feeling," I tell her, and she smiles. "How long have you been watching over me?"

"Decades. I was assigned to be your guardian, told to protect you at all costs, mainly from Elias. But when I was brought back, it was spelled so that you wouldn't be able to see me. I have no idea what's changed, why you can see me now."

"It's gotta be Reyha's new abilities," Trixie says, bending down to pick up the amulet Elias dropped. "This thing must've contained someone else's magic, so instead of stripping your powers, he magnified them. All that extra juice heightened your senses even more."

She searches Elias's body. "Ooh, lookie what I found." She holds up a tiny little book between her thumb and forefinger. "I'm willing to bet this is important." Trixie slips the book into the cup of her bra, and I make a mental note to look that over later—the book, not her breasts. Although, those are stellar too.

"Our boy here did well, all things considered," Vala says, gesturing to Jameson. "He's a keeper."

"I like to think so," I say, smiling over at him.

He returns my gaze and produces a smile of his own.

Vala turns to him. "Thanks for all your help, pretty boy. Couldn't have done it without you."

"Next time, no portals," he says.

"I don't think there's going to be a next time," she says with an air of finality, though I detect a hint of sadness.

I frown. "What do you mean?"

"Elias is dead. My work here is finished. And since the moment he took his last breath, I've felt this strange pull, this tug on where my heart used to be, like something or someone is calling me home. I think it's time to lean in and let go."

I don't want her to leave, but I know she has to.

"Don't be sad," she tells me. "I couldn't ask for a better sendoff."

That one makes me smile through my tears.

"It was good to see you again, Vala," Trixie says. "Blessed be."

"Thanks for everything, Trixie." Vala gives her a subtle nod, and I can tell by her tone that there's a hidden message in there. She floats back a few paces. "Oh, and Rey?"

"Yeah?"

"Get some sleep. You look like hell."

I laugh. "Love you too, Val."

Vala gently fades away, her essence slipping into the cool night breeze and drifting off to wherever she's supposed to go next. All that remains of her now are the memories. Her soul is free. She can finally rest, and that's all that matters.

And the same goes for Jameson, Trixie, and me. We can all rest too.

I walk over to Jameson and take both his hands in mine, looking up at him. "Thank you for coming all this way."

He cups my face in his hands and wipes my tears away, then he leans forward to give me a long, deep kiss. It's a gesture that says so much more than his words ever could. He cares about me. He missed me. And he's relieved I'm okay.

"I'd do it all over again," he swears.

I go in for seconds, pressing my lips against his and thanking my lucky stars that he found me—not just today, but in general. It's strange, I don't have to look over my shoulder or start over in a new place anymore. I'm free to live out my life with Jameson by my side for however long that may be. And he knows I'm a witch, too. Being privy to that knowledge could easily put him in danger, but that's a conversation for another day.

"All right, you two," Trixie says as she places a hand on each of our backs. "I hate to interrupt this touching little moment, but Reyha and I need to heal Mother Nature—stat. We totally trashed her."

We glance at all the chaos and destruction we left in our wake. Broken tree limbs and branches litter the forest floor, and small fires are burning everywhere.

Trixie's right. We have to restore this. The forest heals us, and we heal her.

I mend the trees while Trixie dashes around the scene of the crime, putting out all the fires. Jameson watches in awe as I spell all the heavy limbs and broken branches to float up to their designated spots and magically reattach themselves, the bark fusing as one. It feels good not to have to hide this part of myself from him anymore.

Trixie and I tag team on the giant severed tree, using our combined magic to put it all back together again.

Once we're finished, Trixie dusts all the dirt and debris off her clothes. "Let's get the hell out of here. I'm dying to get back to my man."

"You found him?" I say, surprised.

"More like he found me. This one's legit. Wait till you meet him."

"What's his name?" I ask.

"Donovan. Donovan…something."

I laugh.

"What about Elias's body? Shouldn't we do something with that?" Jameson asks, staring down at the corpse.

"Nah, the forest can have him," I reply.

He's robbed me of enough time and energy. As far as I'm concerned, he deserves to rot while the vultures feast on his flesh.

Jameson nods, and the three of us exit the forest.

"How do you feel?" Trixie asks me.

"Good."

"You're not drained after that fight?"

"No, I could go for round two."

"Man, that must've been some upgrade."

"Speaking of that," I say, pointing to the witch ball in her hand. "Have you changed your mind at all?"

"Oh, most definitely not. I'll be saving this for later. Gotta savor the moment when I absorb his powers." She winks and then stares ahead as we continue to walk side by side. "I still can't believe it. We finally vanquished him. Where do we go from here?"

I take a deep breath, feeling decades of tension melt away, replaced with a newfound peace and inner calm that I haven't known in a hundred years. "Home."

33

FREDERICK

Three days earlier....

"What are we going to do?" Alice asks in a voice that's trying to hide the hysteria of our predicament, as she clutches at her chest, wanting to pull the spell out and away from her precious heart.

Elias has cursed her and I know that no matter what I give him, she's going to die. No way will he let her live or me; neither of us will come out of this clean.

I search for a counter to his curse, but I find nothing. I assume this is his own personal creation and therefore has no counter. He's an asshole like that. His curses are his alone, I'm sure.

I work to create my own counter but to no avail. I hold my wife as we cry together about what comes next. I know if I don't give him what he's after, he'll torture us. Death is bad enough, but long, drawn-out death is far worse. I will not let my darling Alice suffer.

I wish we could run away, but that curse around her heart will remain no matter where we go, and he'll kill her as soon as he sees us gone. Best to do as he commands and get it over with.

I sigh as I rise from our bed, leaving Alice to hug her pillow and stare off into space, trying to wrap her mind around the fact that this is the end of us. I take the amulet and hold it in my hands, turning it over and looking at all sides of it, hating it, hating him, just hating every fucking thing on earth. I grit my teeth and set the amulet on my workbench, knowing I better get to it or worse things will come.

I do this only for my wife and for the hope of her peaceful passing. If I could save her, I would absolutely give my life, but I can't. I know what Elias is like, and I know there's no pity in him, no mercy, no getting through that thick head of his that this is wrong and he should stop what he's doing. There's not a thing in the world that will stop what's about to happen.

I gather herbs and stones, cursed things, dark and evil things that I have in my possession only to protect people from them. I hide the cursed bits of our clan the best I can. I know if I have them then no one else does.

But Elias knew. How, I have no idea, but maybe someone as malevolent as he can feel cursed things of our world. Maybe dark souls call out to other dark souls.

I rub my hands together over the amulet and chant the words of evil and desolation. I say things I swore I'd never speak aloud. I would never take the power of another, but I know how and that is why my wife will die. I can master such things only because I was taught as a last resort by my father, hundreds of years ago. He feared my evil mother would seek me out for my power, but she never did. She died in a battle many years ago, and her powers were caught in a witch ball, hidden from the rest of the witching world.

I sighed in relief when I learned she was gone.

But I still know the things I know. I pick up a bone of a doe; I need something pure for the evil to feast on. I hold it over the amulet as if I'm fanning it, back and forth, chanting the words that make my mouth taste like ash. I surround the amulet with tiny bits of crystal and stone and dead things as I continue on, hating myself for it.

"Frederick?" calls the sweet voice of my wife. It's the only thing that will stop my chanting.

"Yes, love?"

"Stop the spell," she says as she staggers weakly to my work area.

"Darling, you need to be in bed. You must rest up and be strong enough for that spell to be taken off of you," I say, not willing to speak death to my loved one.

"No. I'm going to die. I know it, and so do you. Elias isn't going to let me live, or you for that matter. But, we won't go out on our knees. He's arrogant and foolish. So foolish, I believe, that he won't try out that curse you're creating for him. He'll believe you're so afraid for my life that you'll do what he says, and in most cases, he'd be right, but you can't save me. Nothing can, so I have a proposal for you," she says as she loses her balance and falls into my arms.

I lift her and carry her back to bed, but she holds tight to my arm, forcing me to stay with her.

"Make the spell give his victim more power. Do the opposite of what he wants. Make it our last stand," she whispers as she closes her dark eyes and I stroke her blonde hair, wishing I could save her.

But she's given me the inspiration I lacked. I go back to my bench and clear out all the components for evil and wipe away the spell I had started. I gather the elements of power and force them all into this lovely amulet. I'm going to curse this so hard in the other direction that I hope the witch he's using it on is strong enough to hold it all. I feel so good about this that I laugh to myself.

I'll have to make the incantation simple. I need it to be obvious what he needs to read to make this work because I know I'll be dead before he casts this spell. He wants me to create it and show him how to use it—and then poof, he ends my family.

Or does he?

Once the hex on the amulet is done and my work on the book finished, I create another spell, one to make damn sure my wife and I find each other after he kills us. Whoever dies first will linger until the other is killed, then we will enter that promised afterlife together. That doesn't sound so bad.

Once I'm finished, I kiss my wife goodbye and take one long, last look at her perfection. I put the most beautiful stone I have into her hand and squeeze it tight, making sure it'll still be there when she dies.

I take my stone and stick it in my pocket, hoping I'm quick enough to grab hold of it as I die. It's not the only way this spell will work, but the stones are my last little bit of insurance.

Now, I wait for that miserable excuse for a lifeform to summon me, knowing that he's summoning his own doom.

34

REYHA

It feels good to be home again. Trixie and I whisked through the front door, only to be greeted by Donovan—Rigby! His last name is Rigby. He kept watch over the house and even cleaned the place up while we were gone. Once I saw his face, I immediately recognized him as the guy I ran into in our neighborhood a couple weeks back.

Trixie was right about him; he's her match. The two of them are so connected, so intertwined, they often finish each other's thoughts. It's like they speak their own language. And don't even get me started on their matching auras.

Truth be told, I couldn't be happier for her. She's waited so long for this. I was starting to worry that the universe had redirected her soulmate to someone else, but I realize now it was just waiting for the right time.

When we got back, Trixie wasted no time leveling herself up with Elias's magic. Donovan and I had to hide the witch balls for a few days because she absorbed so much dark energy, but now she's back to her usual spunky self. Thankfully, there don't appear to be any lingering side effects or dark entities hanging around.

I adjust my hat and use my forearm to wipe the sweat from my face as I lean over and continue to patch up the garden, my poor flowerbeds neglected and thirsty and trampled to hell. I whisper a little spell and they gradually rise up from the dirt, looking healthy and vital again.

"Mind if I join you?" a deep voice asks.

Jameson.

I glance up and marvel at this man's beauty. "I'd love that. Grab Trixie's gloves and an extra set of pruning shears from the garage, and I'll put you to work."

"At your service, milady." Jameson grins and disappears.

When he returns, he slips on the gloves and kneels beside me and busies himself with pruning the dwarf lilac bush. It feels good to spend quality time together, doing simple, seemingly mundane tasks. I could stay out here all day and prune plants with him, even if neither of us says a word. That's how I know I'll never get bored of him. He makes the tedious stuff enjoyable.

"Okay, so tell me about this plant," he says, pointing to a shrub that's sporting loads of pink flowers.

"That's oleander—highly toxic to humans. We use that for love spells and purification."

"What about this one?" He points to a plant with tall spikes and purple blooms.

"That's vervain. Great for healing remedies, along with the elderflower."

"And this one?" He points to another set of purple blooms.

"That's monkshood. We use that for invisibility and protection. It works well with the amaranth to prevent physical attacks and ward off those who seek to harm us."

"And the basil? What's that used for?"

"Spaghetti, mostly."

"Of course. Why would I assume anything else?" he teases.

Just then, the door to the house swings open and out prances Trixie with Donovan in tow.

"Where are you two headed?" I ask.

"Gotta run to the store to buy more product so I can whip up a new batch of Rejuvenation for our skincare customers. People are looking dry and deceased out here, and it's not even fall yet. Besides, it's been a couple of weeks since we restocked the site. Backorders are piling up."

"Thank you," I tell her, eternally grateful that she's covering me this week.

Normally it's my job to create the lotions and serums. Trixie handles all the bottling, packaging, and shipping, but she's giving me the week off to recover.

The two sneak off in a hurry, leaving Jameson and me alone.

"You doing okay?" Jameson asks, bringing my attention back to the present.

"Yeah. Better than I thought I'd be. You?"

"Same. It's a lot to take in, but each day is getting easier."

I know exactly what he means, though we're not talking about the same thing. I reach over and grab his hand, giving it a gentle squeeze. "Thank you again for all the trouble you went through to find me."

"It was no trouble at all. If the roles had been reversed, you would've done it for me."

He's right, I would have. But I'm not a mortal chasing down witches and warlocks. Ergo, his sacrifice is greater.

He reaches out and tucks a loose strand of hair behind my ear. "Stay with me tonight?"

I don't know what the future has in store for us, but for once in my life, I'm going to relax and enjoy the moment. A big smile sweeps across my face. "I thought you'd never ask."

35

L E N A

Damn it.

I thought we'd catch Reyha and Elias in the same vicinity at least, but no. I can feel her. She *was* here with him and other wielders of our power, but the lines get fuzzy after that.

There were several witches here, at least six, no question. The buzz of power still lingers. It's quiet but it's here. And its shadow is so strong that it makes my mouth water.

If I can get this power for myself, well, my days of worrying will be at an end. I can keep my coven under control and probably knock over a few other covens, take some more power for myself and so forth. Sounds like a wonderful plan.

I might not have much of my own power anymore, but I have an army of witches who will do whatever I order them to do, considering I'm the head of their community.

I also have a second council I keep off the books.

"Zane, what say you?" I ask.

"Madam, you need to see this," he says, his accent thick Hungarian. He's skinny and lank, but the power inside this unassuming fellow is shocking. And he'll do my will without asking questions.

I walk to the spot where he stands and he bows, pointing to the charred pile of bones before us.

I'm stunned, to say the least. I didn't feel the presence of death. This person was so obliterated that not the slightest bit of their aura is left. It's almost like this person was killed twice.

I pick up a bone, knowing it will be of no consequence. This burned-out corpse is only that of someone who got in Elias's way. A person from the village below who accidentally saw too much. A man out tending sheep or a woman out for a walk from a nearby farm, but the bone burns my hand and I drop it quickly, feeling as if I know now what being electrocuted does to the senses.

This bone belongs to a member of the magical community. I can scarcely believe it. Did he really kill Reyha? Was he able to get past all that love he thought he felt and finish her? It seems so. Her witch balls will be up for grabs and my heart leaps at the thought. I'll be strong again.

"This fellow, there's nothing left of him," Zane says, kicking the bones around, and I break out of my reverie at the word *fellow*.

I walk around the dead guy at my feet and look at every inch of his frame, his leg bones, his pelvis, rib cage, hands, but when I get to his collarbone I feel my fear rise.

I don't want to look at his skull. I know what I'll see. I know what the bones will tell me.

I know already that this is what's left of Elias. I *know* it.

Reyha killed him? She was able to overpower him? It seems unlikely, but here we are.

"His magic was stripped from him, too, Madam," Zane says, running his hands over the black remains.

I take his word and I feel overwhelmed with the idea that Reyha has acquired Elias's power for one of her witch balls. Yet another opportunity missed. But more to be gained when I see her ended.

I walk from the site of Elias's last stand and enter farther into the woods, needing its rejuvenating touch, but nothing will lift the melancholy I feel.

Nothing but a war waged on Reyha and all who support her.

"Zane, call forth your brothers. You leave for America today. Our war begins now."

COMING SOON

BOOK III

LEGACY

ACKNOWLEDGMENTS

CAROL

First, as always, I need to thank God for giving me the skill and the madness to write thousands of words in one sitting in order to get the story out of my head and out to those who read my stuff. Thanks to my children for giving me the will and the desire to be better every single day, whether it's being a better parent or just making a better peanut butter and jelly sandwich. Thank you, boys, for everything. It all means nothing without you. Thanks to the friends who keep me laughing and who support me without questioning why I do what I do. I love you all to death.

LAUREN

Thank you to Andria Flores for editing this manuscript and providing valuable feedback. It was a pleasure to work with you, and you did a wonderful job balancing Carol's style with mine.

Thank you to Vicky Stafford for proofreading this book and offering great suggestions to help elevate our story. I deeply admire your storytelling ability and your creative process. Thank you for inspiring me every single day.

Thank you to our other proofreader, Julia Pratt, for your notes and wonderful attention to detail, and for your infectious enthusiasm.

Thank you to my family and friends, who are always there for me no matter what. I love you all madly, and I couldn't ask for a better tribe.

Thank you to my husband, Ben, for your unwavering support, endless love, and wholehearted acceptance of who I am. So many.

Last but certainly not least, thank you to Carol Sabel Blodgett, my badass partner in crime. You brought so many wonderful ideas and elements to this story; it's the perfect blend of us. One step closer to owning that island…

ABOUT THE AUTHORS

Carol Sabel Blodgett is an author with several books published. Her Moncrief Legends series has just seen its sixth book released. *Wanderer*, *Captive*, *Vanished*, *Revenge*, *Thaddeus*, and *Sacrifice* are all available on Amazon. She has three sons, Alex, Adam, and Drew, who are great writers in their own rights. She helps rescue dogs, maintains friendships with those from childhood while cultivating new ones from adulthood, knowing she is blessed in all her companions. She has more work due out this year.

L.M. Pratt, who also writes romance under the name Lauren Michelle, is an editor by day and a writer by night. She's published two other novels—*Chasing Mia* and *Catching Raven*, available on all platforms. Lauren currently lives in Iowa with her wonderful husband Ben, her son Xander, and a golden retriever named Milo.

FOR UPDATES ON FUTURE PROJECTS, FOLLOW US:

CAROL SABEL BLODGETT
Twitter: @sabelblodgett
Instagram: @carolsabelblodgett
Facebook: Carol Sabel Blodgett

L.M. PRATT
Twitter: L.M. Pratt
Instagram: @laurenmichellepratt
Facebook: Author L.M. Pratt

PURGATORY